IN THE BODYGUARD'S ARMS

BY
LISA CHILDS

This book is produced from independently certified FSC™ paper to ensure responsible forest management.

For more information visit www.harpercollins.co.uk/green

Printed and bound in Spain
by CPI, Barcelona

MILLS
BOON

First Published in Great Britain 2018
By Mills & Boon, an imprint of HarperCollins*Publishers*
1 London Bridge Street, London, SE1 9GF

© 2018 Lisa Childs

ISBN: 978-0-263-26454-8

18-0118

MIX
Paper from
responsible sources

FSC
www.fsc.org
FSC™ C007454

Jordan Mannes stood strong and steady now, unlike her, whose legs still trembled with exhaustion and…

She wasn't sure what she was feeling anymore. Fear. Excitement. The adrenaline rush had yet to leave her; her pulse raced and her skin was flushed.

"You need to let me take you to the clinic," she said. "Or at least try to wash out your eyes."

"No," he said. "There's no time. I have to find the guy who grabbed you." He touched his red face and grimaced. "Did you think I was him—coming back—when you sprayed me?"

"I didn't know who you were," she said. "I wasn't expecting the bodyguard to arrive for a couple of days yet."

"I flew here."

Teddie's skin chilled as a wave of doubt crashed over her. "There's no airport for over a hundred miles, and that doesn't take commercial flights."

"I didn't fly commercial," he said. "I didn't want to waste any time getting here."

Which had been damn lucky for her if he was telling the truth.

If he was who he claimed he was.

Could she trust him?

* * *

Be sure to check out the previous books in the exciting
Bachelor Bodyguards series.

Ever since **Lisa Childs** read her first romance novel (a Mills & Boon story, of course) at age eleven, all she wanted was to be a romance writer. With over forty novels published with Mills & Boon, Lisa is living her dream. She is an award-winning, bestselling romance author. Lisa loves to hear from readers, who can contact her on Facebook, through her website, www.lisachilds.com, or her snail-mail address, PO Box 139, Marne, MI 49435, USA.

For my hero—Andrew Ahearne.
I appreciate your love and support
more than I can say. Thank you for all you
do for us and our family! Love you!

Chapter 1

Fear gripped Jordan "Manny" Mannes—fear like he'd never felt before, not even when he'd been on those top secret missions with his former Marines unit.

He shook his head. "No, I won't take that assignment. No way."

"You don't want to guard a lingerie model?" his boss, Cooper Payne, asked from the end of the long table in the conference room of the Payne Protection Agency franchise he owned. This room and the entire office had been repaired after a recent shoot-out. Redone in dark brick and thick wood, it was a little more bulletproof than all the glass had been.

"Really?" Cooper asked, his blue eyes gleaming with amusement.

Manny didn't think there was anything funny about the assignment. Guarding a model sounded like a nightmare to him and should have sounded like a bad idea to his boss. His guarding a model was like putting the fox in charge of the henhouse. He would be the one getting eaten alive, though.

Sweat broke out on Manny's back, beads trickling down between his shoulder blades, but instead of feeling hot, he felt chilled. "No…"

That would be his worst nightmare: letting himself get distracted because of a pretty face and, since she was a lingerie model, probably a killer body. He knew how shallow he was, that he'd let himself mistake infatuation for something more. Then he'd wind up like the fools from his unit or, worse yet, his hapless family members.

He glanced around the table at the guys with whom he'd served. Lars Ecklund and Dane Sutton were the tallest, most muscular guys he'd ever met. Maybe that was why they had fallen the hardest—so hard that they looked brain damaged. Their eyes glazed like they were drunk. They wore sappy grins nearly as big as they were. They were the "before" pictures.

He glanced farther down the table to the "after"—to Cole Bentler, who'd fallen in love and been betrayed. He didn't look happy; he looked bitter and miserable.

Given Manny's luck, that was how he would wind up—like the "after." Or worse yet, he'd wind up serving like the men in his family: time behind bars.

The Mannes men were legendary for their poor judgment. In women and life decisions. His dad had left his mom for a younger woman he'd later caught cheating on him. That was how Manny had learned, at eight years old, what a crime of passion was.

Then there were crimes of stupidity, like his brother

letting his pretty girlfriend talk him into robbing a liquor store. Jeremy had gone to prison while Manny had gone off to the Marines. He'd enlisted in the hopes of escaping the family curse.

He had felt safer carrying out dangerous missions overseas than he did here. He had had fewer distractions over there.

"No, absolutely not," he said. "Send Cole." Cole wasn't going to fall in love with anyone ever again—not after how his heart had been crushed. "Or Nikki…"

Lars's pale blue eyes dimmed slightly with disappointment. He'd just moved in with his fiancée a few weeks ago; of course he wouldn't want to be separated from her.

"Or borrow a bodyguard from one of your brothers," Manny suggested. Each of the Payne brothers had their own franchise of Payne Protection now, and when the need arose, they all worked together.

"Why would I do that when you're available?" Cooper asked.

"I—I'm not available," Manny said. "I'm taking that other case."

"What other case?" Cooper asked, his brow furrowing with confusion.

"Protecting Ted…" He couldn't think of the guy's last name right away. He'd only heard it mentioned when he'd overheard their receptionist transferring the call to Cooper a few days ago. But as Cooper opened his mouth to speak again, he remembered the name and interrupted. "Plummer. I want that job," he said. "I'll protect Ted Plummer."

Cooper shook his head. "You don't know—"

"I don't care," Manny said. "I don't need to know

all the details. I know how this bodyguard business works. The guy's in danger. I'll protect him."

"But the job's in the Upper Peninsula," Cooper said. "It's at a very secluded cabin."

And Manny preferred cities like Atlanta, where he'd grown up. Hot, bustling cities. He shuddered slightly. But then, maybe being secluded was a good thing. It would make it easier to protect old Ted from whatever the threat was to his safety, and it would make it harder for Manny to find some woman to fall for—like his idiot friends and family had.

"That's the job I want," Manny said. "I want to protect Ted Plummer."

Cooper leaned back for a moment and studied Manny while everyone else studied Cooper. There was a strange energy in the room, but Manny figured it was because none of the guys were used to him acting like this. He was usually the easygoing one of the bunch. He did what was asked of him; he didn't fight for an assignment.

Until today. He wanted this job. He needed to get away from River City for a while. And most of all, he needed to get away from his friends who'd fallen in love. Just a few days ago he'd helped Dane pick out a ring for the woman he hoped to marry.

He shuddered at the memory and with the concern that if he stayed too close to all this happiness, it might get to him. It might make him think that he could have what they had. And that just wasn't possible. Nobody in his family had ever had a successful relationship.

Finally Cooper nodded. "Ted Plummer is all yours."

Manny should have been happy, but for some reason a sick feeling rushed over him. He felt light-headed and dizzy for a moment. But then the feeling passed.

"Go pack," Cooper advised. "You have a plane to catch."

"I can fly myself there," Manny said.

"Payne Protection doesn't have planes," Cooper said. "But it might not be a bad investment since you and Cole both have your pilot's licenses."

"You can take mine," Cole Bentler almost sheepishly offered. "I have one at the River City airstrip." Bentler had money but didn't like to admit it.

Maybe he thought his friends would act differently if they knew. Like maybe Manny wouldn't pay his half of the rent for the apartment they shared or something. But Manny didn't care about money. It obviously hadn't made Cole happy.

Love hadn't made him happy, either.

So Manny wasn't going to take any chances. Somebody else could protect the lingerie model. He was going to be perfectly happy with old Ted.

The door closed behind Manny with a sharp snap as he rushed from the conference room. But Cooper was the only one watching the door. Everyone else was still staring at him.

"You're not going to tell him?" Cole Bentler asked.

Cooper snorted and then called him on his hypocrisy. "You volunteered your plane but no other information."

"But you're the boss," Cole said.

Pride swelled in Cooper's chest. Yes, he was the boss—of his own security agency. But just because he was the boss didn't mean he couldn't have some fun. The laughter he'd been suppressing escaped.

Lars and Dane erupted, too—deep chuckles filling the room.

Cole just shook his head, but he was grinning as he warned, "He's going to be so pissed."

"It's his own damn fault for not knowing her name," Dane remarked. "When we started boot camp, he had a pinup picture of her that he was going to put in his locker."

But boot camp wasn't like high school; there were no lockers. Just stiff cots and scratchy blankets and muscle-aching, soul-breaking hard work.

"I don't think he was interested in her name," Lars remarked with another guffaw.

"It's not like he ever expected to meet her," Cole said. He shook his head again.

"But how can he not know that Ted Plummer is really Teddie Plummer, the supermodel?" Cooper asked. "Even though her career has slowed down recently, her name is still in every tabloid."

The guys stared at him again like they had during the meeting—silently—until Lars asked, "How the hell do you know that?"

Heat rushed to Cooper's face, but he just shrugged. "My wife reads the tabloids. They're always lying around the house. I'm surprised Manny wouldn't know."

Manny was notorious for not being able to keep a secret except the ones that would endanger all their lives if revealed. Those he kept.

Cole snorted. "We don't have any tabloids lying around our apartment."

He and Manny shared an attic apartment in some old downtown house. They were the ultimate odd couple. Manny talked incessantly while Cole was reticent.

Manny had grown up in poverty while Cole had money. Cooper certainly didn't pay him enough to afford a private plane.

"He has no idea who she is," Cole added.

"He's going to find out soon," Lars warned him. "You're going to have to send up someone else when he turns around and flies right back."

Cooper shook his head now. "You all heard him. He demanded the assignment. So he has to protect her and find out who the hell's stalking her."

Teddie Plummer was in danger. And protecting her would put Manny in danger, too. Even though he was an excellent bodyguard, he should have been briefed. But he had been so anxious to leave, he really hadn't given Cooper the chance.

Or at least, that was what Cooper wanted to believe—that Manny hadn't given him the chance and he and Teddie Plummer would be safe.

The supermodel had called the Payne Protection Agency because someone was stalking her. He'd escalated from sending her threatening notes to breaking into her penthouse and trying to grab her in the park. This person was obsessed with her, so obsessed that he wasn't likely to give up until one of them was dead.

She was dead.

Teddie had never been so tired. Not even after twelve-hour photo shoots had she ever been this exhausted. She had hiked miles through the pine trees and rock formations of the Porcupine Mountains Park. Then she'd kayaked across the clear blue surface of the Lake in the Clouds. The muscles in her arms burned. The muscles in her legs burned. She ached all over.

But as exhausted as she was, nervous energy filled her. The snap of every twig along the trail had her jumping. And despite seeing no other hikers for over an hour, she felt as if she was being watched.

She glanced around but could see no one through the thick branches of the pine trees lining the narrow trail. This wasn't part of the park anymore; it was the trail that led from her property to the park.

She would be back soon to the cabin. She would be able to lock herself inside and pull all the blinds to make sure nobody could see her.

Another twig snapped, and a startled cry slipped through her lips. The noise was too loud for it to have been a squirrel or chipmunk. Something bigger was out there.

Something human?

She shivered and quickened her pace. Her legs ached with each step, but she ignored the pain. She ignored everything but the fear.

The fear had kept her alive the past several weeks. She'd been able to outrun her stalker before—in Central Park. But that had been on neatly paved running trails. And he had nearly caught her then. He'd grabbed her arm.

She could feel his crushing grip even now. The bruises from his fingers had turned yellow on her forearm. If she hadn't kicked...

If she hadn't screamed...

What would he have done to her?

All those things he threatened in the letters he sent her? All those damn letters with cut-up images of her face—of her body...

She shivered despite the sweat that had dampened

her clothes, or maybe because of it. The temperature had begun to drop along with the sun. Dusk had begun to gather on the trail, casting ominous shadows. Of the trees? Or of the man who always found her no matter where she hid?

Of course it had been easy for him to find her in the city—despite all the people. The paparazzi followed her and posted enough photos of her day that it was easy to know where she went and what she did.

But he had found her at her mama's house, too, in the hills of Kentucky. He'd gotten inside the small house her mother had insisted on keeping even though Teddie had wanted to buy her a bigger one once the modeling contracts had started coming in. He had been in Teddie's childhood bedroom, touching her things, cutting them up.

She shuddered as she thought of that, of how the space where she had once felt safe had been violated. Of how her mama could have been hurt.

But Mama was tough. She'd been only seventeen when she'd had Teddie. The boy who'd gotten her pregnant had wanted nothing to do with her anymore, not once he'd gotten what he'd wanted from the girl he and his jock friends had all called trailer trash. Mama's parents had already abandoned her, so she'd been living with her grandmother in a trailer park. Once her grandmother had died, Mama had raised Teddie alone in the little house she'd used the small inheritance from her grandmother to buy.

Mama had worked two jobs to keep them fed and clothed. And she'd also worked hard to keep them safe. So when they had returned home from eating out and discovered the intruder, Mama had pulled a gun from her purse and fired it.

If only she'd hit him…

But she'd broken the window instead. And the masked intruder had jumped through it and escaped. A slight smile curved Teddie's lips as she thought of Mama's fierceness.

She probably didn't have to worry about the stalker bothering her mother again. But she hadn't wanted to take the chance. So Teddie had insisted on leaving.

She had bought this place up north sight unseen. She'd fallen in love with the area a few years ago after a friend had brought her to the area to hike. She'd fallen in love with the trees and trails and water. She had felt so at peace here.

But not anymore.

Another twig snapped, and she gasped. Her heart was beating fast and hard, and she was beginning to pant, not from the exertion but from the fear that pressed on her lungs.

She hoped it was a bear. She'd seen them before in the woods. They'd left her alone. They hadn't been any more interested in her than she'd been in them.

But now…

Now she felt as if she were being followed. Stalked.

And again, she couldn't help but think it was him. That *he* had found her.

Maybe she should have taken the gun as Mama had suggested. Since she had little experience firing one, she'd thought it might be as dangerous for her to have the weapon as it was for her to have the stalker. So she'd taken her mother's other suggestion instead.

She'd hired the Payne Protection Agency.

Mama had seen a feature about them on a nightly news broadcast, about all the people they'd protected from harm or death, and all the cases they'd solved. If anyone could help her, they could.

But could they?

The police hadn't been able to help Teddie. Not the big city departments in New York or LA or even the local force down in Blackwater, Kentucky. She doubted the Payne Protection Agency could do what no one else had.

She doubted they could stop her stalker. But she would give them a chance. Cooper Payne, the owner, had tried to convince her to come to River City in the Lower Peninsula of Michigan, where their office was. But she'd refused. The drive was too long, and Teddie could not fly anymore. She couldn't handle the fear, not of crashing but of being trapped in a confined space with her stalker. What if he were on the flight? She wouldn't be able to get away from him a plane.

So Cooper had told her that he would send a bodyguard up to her. She didn't expect him anytime soon, though. Even if he flew, there was no airport nearby. He'd have to drive part of the way—if he would be able to find her at all at the remote cabin.

Another twig snapped, this one closer. If it was a bear, she was supposed to lie down and play dead. If she ran, it would chase her. And she wouldn't be able to outrun the bear like she had her stalker.

But instinct had her running, her legs burning as she sprinted along the trail. She knew it wasn't a bear following her. She knew it was him. And he was too close.

Finally the trail widened, the trees along it not as thick as they had been between the park and her property. The darkness was falling, casting shadows so deep she couldn't see where she was going.

She glanced over her shoulder to see where she'd been and whether he emerged from the narrow trail behind her. She didn't want him to follow her here, to the cabin where she'd finally felt safe.

She was so close to it. She turned toward it, where her legs were instinctively carrying her. The muscles were numb now, all sensation gone from them. She had to will herself to keep moving. As she neared the small structure with its cedar siding and big windows, she felt a flash of relief. And then a flash of panic.

A light glowed inside it, burning behind the blinds she'd kept closed since she'd arrived. Had she turned on a lamp before she'd left?

She had awakened after dawn. With sunshine streaming through the tall windows in the peak of the A-frame, where blinds weren't necessary for privacy, she wouldn't have needed a light. And she hadn't intended to be out as long as she'd been, so she probably wouldn't have thought she would need one to see her way back home.

But if she hadn't left that light on, then someone else must have turned it on. She began to slow her pace. Then she heard it again—another crack of a twig or limb breaking behind her.

Was she running from danger or straight toward it?

Chapter 2

Where the hell was Ted Plummer? Manny couldn't protect someone he couldn't find. Cooper had given him the name of the township where the guy's cabin was and an address, which was really more of a property parcel number than a street address. Since Manny's phone barely got reception up here, it wasn't like he'd been able to plug it into his GPS. He had no idea he was at the right cabin, not that there had been many other ones to choose from in this area.

So he probably had found the right place. But if he had, where the hell was Ted?

Was Manny too late? There was no body, no blood spattered around. No signs of a struggle.

Of course, if Manny had had this much trouble finding Ted, the stalker probably had, as well. It wasn't like Ted would have given that person his property address.

What the hell was Ted that he had a stalker? Manny remembered now that the reception had told Cooper that *Teddie Plummer* needed a bodyguard. He'd been the one who'd shortened it to Ted. Teddie Plummer sounded like an accountant. Maybe for the IRS? And someone he'd audited wanted revenge?

No. A tax accountant probably wouldn't call himself Teddie. He would be a Theodore. No. Teddie sounded like…

Like what?

Manny felt a prickle of unease, and it wasn't just because he'd found the cabin empty when he'd shown up. And it was getting dark…

After opening the unlocked door, he'd flipped on a light. But nobody had fallen asleep on the couch. Or in the bed in the loft. In fact, the bed with the drawers beneath it was so neatly made with a plaid comforter and navy sheets that it looked as if it hadn't been slept in. Maybe he hadn't found the right place after all.

The cabin looked spotless, not a plate or glass sitting out on the wooden counter or lying in the black hammered farmhouse sink. The only things lying around were books. Could Teddie be a professor? Was a student stalking him, wanting revenge over a bad grade or something?

But when Manny picked up one of the books, a paper fell out. It looked like notes a student would make, not the professor. And the handwriting was very neat with a feminine flourish to the letters that increased Manny's uneasy feeling. Was it just that Teddie had another person's book, another person's notes?

Or was there something else going on?

Manny shouldn't have been so quick to leave the

conference room. He should have let Cooper brief him on the situation with Teddie Plummer, so Manny could have found out who the hell Teddie was.

Because that name sounded vaguely familiar to him now.

So familiar that Manny had a bad feeling not just that something had happened to Teddie Plummer but that something was about to happen to him.

Something bad was about to happen. Teddie knew it. Even though she was close—so close that she could see the light burning inside her cabin—she wasn't going to reach it in time. She wasn't sure that it would be any safer in there, anyway, as a shadow passed behind the blinds. A hulking shadow. Whoever had broken into her place was big, so big she doubted she would be able to fight him off.

She couldn't turn around, either. Someone was behind her. She was certain of it. Too many twigs kept snapping while brush rustled. Someone or something was behind her. So she had to keep running forward, not to the cabin but beyond it to the big shed where she'd hidden her Jeep.

But the keys were inside the house, hanging on a hook by the back door she was certain she'd locked. How had the intruder broken in? And if he was inside, who was chasing her?

Had she had two stalkers this entire time? No wonder it seemed as though she'd never been able to get away from him. That he always found her wherever she was.

Despite the sweat dampening her clothes, she shivered as her blood chilled. She couldn't fight off two of them. And she might not be able to outrun them, either.

Without the keys, she wouldn't be able to start the Wrangler and use it to escape. And she wasn't certain how much longer she could run. The numbness had left her muscles to leave a burning pain. She felt like her ligaments were on fire and about to tear.

But she couldn't stop. Now she didn't hear just the snap of the twigs or the rustle of the brush. She heard footsteps—pounding against the ground. Whoever was behind her was gaining on her.

And she was so close to the cabin where that shadow lurked behind the blinds. She was trapped with no hope of escaping. Would this be how it ended?

If only she had hired the Payne Protection Agency sooner...

Then she wouldn't be alone facing the greatest danger of her life. The bodyguard would already be with her instead of somewhere en route. But Teddie wasn't entirely helpless. While she didn't have the gun that her mother had offered to lend her, she always carried a canister of pepper spray with her.

She had thought she would be safe from the stalker here in the Upper Peninsula of Michigan. Out of habit, though, she'd clipped the canister on her belt before she'd left for her hike to protect herself from a bear.

She really hoped that was what was following her.

But she heard no growl, just the deep pant of labored breathing as the distance closed between her predator and his prey. Before she could unclip the canister from her belt, a hand caught her hair, jerking her head back.

She whirled around to face the monster.

* * *

Manny had searched the cabin again, which didn't take long since the structure was small. The kitchen consisted of a short refrigerator, a two-burner stove, that farmhouse sink and a couple of cupboards. The bathroom was nearly as tiny—a stand-up shower squeezed in the corner between a pedestal sink and a toilet. The bedroom was the loft. The biggest room was the open living area. There was an overstuffed couch, an old trunk for a coffee table, and a small secretary-type desk in front of the windows with the closed blinds.

He'd pulled open the drawers beneath that bed and what he'd found had confirmed his fears. He walked back to the desk and that paper with the notes. The handwriting was definitely feminine.

He noticed a folder sticking out from beneath one of the textbooks. When he opened the folder, his breath caught with a gasp.

There weren't notes in the folder, at least not notes taken from a textbook. These notes were scrawled in black marker across cut-up photos. They were threats.

I'm going to mess up your beautiful face...

And he had. The face in the photo had been scraped off, leaving only the body clad in a camisole. Even without the face, Manny recognized the body.

It was everywhere. *She* was everywhere. Or at least, she had been until the past few months. He hadn't thought much of it at the time. For a model, her career had been long, probably spanning nearly a decade and a half. But since she'd started modeling young, she wasn't that old—not old enough to really retire. Now he knew why she'd dropped out of the spotlight. Because of this...

The threats.

There were more photos. Most were missing her face. The rest had other body parts cut out. The notes contained so much hate. So much madness.

He shuddered at the venom, and his skin chilled with fear for her. With dread.

Where the hell was she?

Where was Teddie Plummer?

When he'd searched the cabin again, he'd found a key ring hanging by the unlocked door. Unless she had another set, she probably hadn't driven away. But where was the Jeep?

With another shudder, he dropped that folder back onto the desk. Then he headed toward the back door. He was just reaching for the handle when he heard it, the bloodcurdling scream of terror.

Pulling his gun from his holster, he threw open the door and rushed outside into the all-encompassing blackness. Born and raised in cities, he'd only been anywhere this dark while on missions. Usually street lamps illuminated his way. But now he couldn't see where he was going. So he tripped on the steps leading off the deck.

His breath escaped in an oath as he struck the ground, hard. Twigs and roots tore at his clothes. It was so damn dark. He had a light on his gun. But if he flipped it on, he would lose the element of surprise. Whoever was out there—whoever had caused that scream—would see him coming.

But he wouldn't be able to find Teddie without the light. So he regained his feet and flipped on the switch, sweeping the flashlight beam and the barrel of the gun around the woods surrounding the cabin.

Even with it burning along with the glow shining through the blinds of the cabin's windows, the shadows were thick. No stars even shone in the sky—not that he could see much of the sky through the thick branches of all of the trees.

Some of those branches moved. And leaves and grass rustled. No breeze stirred. The air was cold and damp and stagnant. It wasn't the wind blowing those branches around; it was something. Or someone.

He opened his mouth to call out, but again, he wasn't certain what the situation was. Had Teddie's stalker found her? Or was Teddie even here?

He couldn't be sure she had been staying here any longer. Maybe she had a second set of keys for the Jeep. Or maybe the Jeep wasn't even hers.

He couldn't imagine a supermodel driving a Jeep or staying in that rustic little cabin, either. She had to be a millionaire, at least. For years she had modeled every swimsuit and lingerie brand on the market. He'd even had a poster of her that he'd brought with him to boot camp.

How the hell hadn't he recognized her name?

The guys must have been laughing their asses off at him being so clueless about who she was. And when he'd insisted on taking the assignment, he could just imagine their reactions.

He could not imagine what might be out in those woods, in the dark. Maybe that hadn't even been a human scream. Maybe it had been some animal.

Because he didn't know the reason for the scream,

he held his silence, which any of his friends would have said was unusual for him. Except on missions.

On missions and about missions, he knew to stay quiet. Just like they had all stayed quiet when he had mistaken Teddie for a man. Cooper—of all of them—should have at least given him a heads-up. He was the boss now.

But then, he guessed Cooper had kind of tried. Manny hadn't given him much of an opportunity. He'd been so insistent on taking this case, on staying away from all damsels in distress.

If that scream had come from Teddie, she was definitely in distress. But where the hell was she?

The voice, or whatever it was, had sounded so close. He walked in circles around the cabin, swinging the beam on his gun in ever-widening circles. The beam glanced off tree trunks and brush. The cabin had no yard, just a thinner version of the woods that surrounded the property.

If she was still staying here, what the hell had she been doing outside this late? She'd put herself in danger, not just from her stalker but also from whatever wild animals lived in the area. Bears? Wolves? Mountain lions? He had no idea what could be out there. If any of those things were, he didn't blame her for screaming.

He opened his mouth to call out to her, but then his beam glanced off something on the ground. He moved the flashlight back so the beam took the same path. The shadow was crumpled between two trees, lying lifelessly.

Was it a person? Or a pile of brush?

He stepped closer, and the beam illuminated clothing. The fabric was a shiny blue material, like some kind of workout apparel. He hurried forward now as he noticed the curls, the profusion of bright red ones spilled over the clothing and onto the ground.

Twigs and dirt were matted in her hair. What the hell had happened to her?

"Teddie?" Her name escaped his lips on a rasp of concern. He had to know if she was all right. He leaned over her, but she was facedown on the ground.

He could see only her clothes and her tangled hair. Could he even be certain it was her? He remembered the hair—not just from the desecrated photos he'd found in the cabin, but from memories of all the images he'd seen of her. That he'd had of her.

If she knew, she'd probably think he was a stalker, too. But he never would have desecrated those photos. He never would have written such horrific threats.

Only someone truly sick could have written such things. As he crouched down closer to her, he swept his flashlight and barrel around the woods near them.

Was that creep out there? Waiting to strike again?

Manny was tempted to squeeze the trigger, to fire a few shots and hope he hit the son of a bitch. But none of the trees or brush moved or rustled now.

Whatever had been out there was gone.

Was Teddie gone, too?

He reached out and closed his free hand over her shoulder. She was slender but there was muscle beneath his fingertips, too. That was what had always been so damn sexy about her. She had never looked like she starved herself like so many other models did. She was curvy but fit.

Beautiful but natural.

She'd had no breast implants or lip augmentation. Everything about her had been real. She was the girl next door if the girl next door was drop-dead gorgeous.

Dead…

Damn, he hoped she wasn't—for so many reasons, the primary one being that he would have failed his first solo assignment before it even began.

He drew in a deep breath, bracing himself, before he rolled her toward him. Her hair was tangled across her face, but he could still see the heart shape of her face, the pointy chin and wide cheekbones.

Her eyes—which he remembered being a clear and crisp green—were closed. Some of her hair was tangled in her thick lashes. And dirt was smeared across her forehead and along one cheek.

His breath escaped as he uttered a ragged sigh. At the very least she was unconscious. At the worst, dead. He reached now for her neck to check for a pulse, and his hand shook slightly as he pushed aside her hair.

Her skin was silky and damp and cold beneath his fingertips. Was she…?

He moved his fingers again and finally felt it, the leap of her pulse. She was alive, her pulse pounding madly beneath his fingertips.

He expelled another breath—of relief. "Thank God…"

When he glanced down, he found her eyes open and staring up at him. Her green eyes—so vivid even in the faint glow of the flashlight beam—were wide with fear.

Of course, he was holding a gun on her. She had every reason to be afraid, especially since she must have just been attacked.

"Don't be scared," he told her.

"I'm not," she said, her voice sharp as the fear turned to anger.

Before he could say anything more, he started choking and sputtering as she sprayed a canister right in his face. He couldn't breathe, and his eyes and face burned.

His vision blurred, so it was hard to focus. But as he turned away from her, he caught a sign of movement again—in the trees and the brush as twigs snapped and the leaves rustled. Whoever had attacked her wasn't gone. He'd only been watching, probably for his opportunity to attack again.

Manny had thought he'd failed her once. Now he might fail her again, but this time it was her damn fault for blinding him.

Chapter 3

Teddie choked and sputtered as the pepper spray wafted back into her face. Her eyes and nose stung painfully while her skin burned. She'd had no choice but to spray him.

The man had a gun, one he had been pointing right at her. This must have been the man from the cabin. He was bigger than the one who'd caught her in the dark, pulling her hair to stop her from running.

That man hadn't stopped her from fighting. She'd kicked and clawed and screamed. But he hadn't relented until this man had run from the cabin—or vaulted from it. Then the first man had released her and run off into the woods. Would he have done that if the two men were working together?

She didn't know whom to trust, especially when she'd trusted so many of the wrong people in the past.

That was why she'd dropped out of the public eye—because she'd had no idea which eyes belonged to her stalker.

Still on the ground, she scrambled away from the big man with the gun. Her eyes streaming, she crawled like a crab toward the cabin. The door onto the back porch stood open. She could grab the keys to the Jeep. She could drive away—if she could see.

Not only couldn't she see but she also could barely stand. She tried to regain her footing, but her legs folded beneath her. She dropped to the ground again. Before she could get back up, a hand closed around her arm.

She'd dropped the damn canister after she'd released the pepper spray. There probably hadn't been any left anyway. But she needed something to protect her. This hand was big and strong, bigger and stronger than the one that had gripped her hair and jerked her to the ground.

This man could easily hurt her if he wanted to, and after she sprayed him, he probably wanted to hurt her badly. She was still tempted to fight him the way she'd fought the other man. But this guy had that gun, which was why she'd played dead until he'd gotten close enough for her to use the spray. She knew, just like she hadn't outrun the other man, that she wouldn't have been able to outrun a bullet.

Instead of hurting her, this man helped her up. "Get in the cabin," he urged her. "Lock yourself inside. I checked it already. It's clear. He wouldn't have been able to get around us to get in there."

He sounded like he really wanted to help her—when he should have been furious with her. And yet she couldn't be sure he wasn't just manipulating her. Could she trust him?

She did need to get to the cabin—to her Jeep keys. Maybe by the time she got there, her vision would be clearer. But as she started forward, she stumbled, her legs still too weak to hold her. She'd already been physically exhausted when she'd been forced to run for her life. It was no wonder her muscles were protesting now.

The man caught her again, lifting her easily from the ground. He swung her up in his arms, but he stumbled, too, as he climbed the steps of the small porch to the back door.

Judging from the mammoth size of his arms and shoulders and chest, he wasn't struggling with her weight. Like her, he had to be struggling to see. He made it up the steps and through the open back door. His shoulder struck the jamb, but that might have been just because of how wide his shoulders were.

She'd slung her arm around his shoulders just to steady herself. It wasn't as if she had to hang on. He wasn't about to drop her.

He had one arm under her legs, the other around her back. His arms were hard—like his shoulders and his chest—all sculpted muscles. She would have thought he was carved from rock—if not for his warmth. He wasn't a statue; he was a man.

She needed to wriggle down to break free of his grasp. In the hand of the arm beneath her legs, he still held his gun, the barrel pointed down. The flashlight beam shone like a spotlight on the hardwood floor. What if he pointed the gun at her again?

She didn't have the pepper spray to defend herself.

But she was beginning to believe she hadn't needed to use it.

"Who are you?" she asked as she stared up at his face.

Even with his spray-reddened eyes and skin, he was handsome. His complexion was tan, but that might have been more from nature than the sun. His hair was black, and his eyes were dark, too, but for the red rimming the deep brown irises. He was probably the same age she was: thirty. If they'd ever met before, she would have remembered meeting him.

"Jordan Mannes," he said. "I'm the bodyguard from the Payne Protection Agency."

She gasped in shock and regret. She had maced the man sent to protect her.

"And you're Teddie Plummer?" He asked it like he was wishing she wasn't but afraid she was.

She could understand his not recognizing her if he were familiar with her photographs. She didn't look anything like her pictures right now with her baggy clothes and her hair all dirty and tangled around her face.

She nodded. "Yes, I'm Teddie."

He emitted a short sigh. Of disappointment?

Although she couldn't blame him for not wanting to protect someone who had hurt him.

"Are you okay?" he asked. "You're not hurt?"

She nodded again.

Then he released her and turned back for the door. "And make damn sure you lock it this time," he admonished her. "I found it unlocked when I first got here."

Her breath caught, and she shook her head. He had to be wrong. This had happened at her mama's house. They had been certain they'd locked the door when they'd left for dinner. But when they'd returned, the door had been unlocked.

"It was locked," she insisted. She remembered checking it twice after she'd closed it behind herself. "I always lock the doors."

He shook his head now. "It wasn't when I showed up earlier. So make sure you lock it behind me when I leave."

"You're leaving?" Not that she could blame him after what she'd done to him.

"Somebody's out there, right?" he asked as he looked over his shoulder at her. "That's why you screamed?"

She shuddered as she remembered that hand in her hair, jerking her head back. "Yes. Someone was chasing me through the woods." Her voice cracked with a resurgence of the fear she'd felt when she'd been running, trying to escape him. "And then he caught me."

"Did you recognize him?"

She shook her head. "It all happened so fast," she explained. "He caught me from behind, but when he jerked me around, I couldn't see his face. He had a ski mask on..." So the pepper spray probably wouldn't have affected him—had she had time to shoot the contents of the canister in his face.

"You're sure you're not hurt?" Jordan asked.

"N-no," she stammered. She wasn't physically harmed. But she might have been in shock. No. If she were in shock, she would have been numb. And she was feeling too much now: too much achy pain from overexerting herself and too much fascination with her bodyguard. "I'm fine."

"Good," he said, "because now I'm going to try to catch him. He couldn't have gotten very far yet."

"No," she agreed. "I kicked him—hard." She was surprised he'd been able to move at all, let alone run, when Jordan had rushed out of the cabin.

The bodyguard's mouth curved into a slight grin that Teddie couldn't help but find sexy. He had sensual-looking lips. "Good," he said again, his deep voice even deeper with satisfaction. "Then he probably didn't get far at all."

"But how will you find him?" she asked. "You can't see." She couldn't, and not as much of the spray had gotten in her eyes and face as in his. How was he even standing?

When the volunteer in her self-defense class had been sprayed, the young man had writhed around on the floor in agony until they'd taken him to the ER.

Jordan Mannes stood strong and steady now, unlike her. Her legs still trembled with exhaustion and...

She wasn't sure what she was feeling anymore. Fear. Excitement. The adrenaline rush had yet to leave her, her pulse raced and her skin was flushed. But maybe that was just from the spray—or from how easily Jordan Mannes had carried her.

She shook her head, trying to clear it. Too many sleepless nights and too much fear had taken its toll on her senses. She was losing them.

"You need to let me take you to the clinic," she said. "Or at least try to wash out your eyes."

"No," he said. "There's no time. I have to find the guy who grabbed you." He touched his red face and grimaced. "Did you think I was him—coming back—when you sprayed me?"

"I didn't know who you were," she said. "I wasn't expecting the bodyguard to arrive for a couple of days yet."

"I flew here."

Her skin chilled as a wave of doubt crashed over her. "There's no airport for over a hundred miles and that doesn't take commercial flights."

"I didn't fly commercial," he said. "I didn't want to waste any time getting here."

Which had been damn lucky for her if he was telling the truth.

If he was who he claimed he was.

Could she trust him?

"I'm going to check around outside." He opened and closed the door behind himself before she could protest any further. But through the door, he shouted, "Lock it!"

He was worried about her safety. But what about his own? Not being able to see, he could walk right into danger before he even realized it, kind of like when he had rolled her over and she had pepper-sprayed him.

A pang of regret and concern struck her heart. She wished she hadn't hurt him. And she hoped he would not get hurt even worse.

"Be careful," she called out through the door as she locked it. But she suspected that her warning was too late. That he was already gone.

Whatever was going to happen to Jordan Mannes would happen, and even though she wouldn't be the one doing it this time, it would still be her fault because that madman out there was after her.

Jordan Mannes was only doing his job.

* * *

Over the past few years as a bodyguard, Cooper Payne had heard fear in the voices of many women. Hell, even as a Marine he had heard it—in the voices of friends' families, in his own family.

He heard fear now in Teddie Plummer's voice as she spoke through the speaker on his cell phone. "I think he's been out there too long," she said. "But I haven't heard any gunshots."

"Why would he be shooting?" Cooper asked with concern. "Who would he be shooting at?"

"At the man who attacked me," she said. "Mr. Mannes went back out to see if he could find him. But he can't see…"

It was late. And in the UP, it would be especially dark. "He has a flashlight—"

"Yes," she said. "But he still won't be able to see."

Cooper's head began to pound. Not only was she afraid, but she was also so distraught she wasn't making sense anymore. "He will be able to with the flashlight—"

"He can't see because I pepper-sprayed him earlier."

A curse slipped through Cooper's lips. What the hell kind of situation had he sent his friend into?

Before Cooper had started his own branch of the Payne Protection Agency, his brother Logan had tried to send him off on an assignment to protect some reality star who claimed to have a stalker. She'd made up the whole thing just to get publicity to launch a film career.

Was that what Teddie Plummer was up to? Theatrics in order to get into the theater?

"I didn't think he would be here already," she explained. "I didn't expect the bodyguard you sent to get here for at least another day or two."

"He flew in," Cooper said.

"He got here just in time," Teddie said, and her breath rattled the phone as her fear increased. "I was coming back from a hike when someone chased me through the woods. He had caught me. If Jordan hadn't rushed out when I screamed…"

If she was this good an actress, she would not have needed to stage any publicity stunts to break into movies. She couldn't be faking the terror Cooper heard now.

"He's been out there too long," she murmured again. "Can you send someone else up here?"

Cooper knew that Cole would go. He would leave in a minute even though he would have to borrow someone else's plane since Manny had his. But with the fog that had just rolled into River City, Cooper suspected all flights would be grounded.

"Nobody would get there in time now," Cooper said. If Manny were in danger right now…

"Then I'll go out there," she said. And he could hear the deep breath she drew in to brace herself.

"No!" Cooper said. "The guy already tried to grab you once. If you go back out there…" and if he had already taken out Manny, then there would be no one to protect her.

Damn it, he should not have sent Manny off alone on this assignment. Cooper had had no idea just how dangerous it was. And unfortunately, neither had Manny.

He had been gone too long. The son of a bitch could have circled around the woods and gone back to the cabin. If she'd been telling the truth, if she had locked the door when she'd left earlier, then the bastard must have a key.

Because the lock hadn't looked picked. The jamb hadn't been broken. No. If she had locked the door, then someone had just let himself inside, and he could have done it again the minute Manny had walked out and left her alone and unprotected.

But he'd had to check out the brush he'd seen moving right after Teddie had pepper-sprayed him. He hadn't found anyone hiding in those trees, not that he was certain he'd searched in the right place. All the damn trees and brush looked the same to him.

What he could see of them…

His eyes kept streaming as the spray continued to burn them. He blinked repeatedly and peered through lids that felt swollen and raw. Damn it.

Everything looked the same. He wasn't sure where he'd been or even where the cabin was now. A light shone in the distance, beyond the trees in which he found himself. Was that light glowing from the cabin? Or another house?

He hadn't seen any other homes along this road when he'd driven the motorcycle he had rented from the private airstrip to here. He'd had no idea then if he was heading in the right direction. But her cabin had been the only one he'd found. Not that there couldn't be others set farther back in the woods.

This was bad.

There were no street lamps here because there were no streets. No sidewalks. He had no idea where he was or how to get back to her. He rubbed his eyes again and tried to focus.

He needed to get back to the cabin. He needed to

make sure she was safe. He should have at least left her the gun for protection. She might be able to hit her target. He wasn't certain that he would be able to.

As Manny moved toward that light, it wavered. Maybe it only appeared that way because of his eyes, though. They continued to burn, but it wasn't just from the spray anymore. As he walked closer, he realized the light came from a fire burning inside a circle of rocks. He'd stumbled upon someone's campsite.

He hadn't walked that far, so whoever was camping here was close to the cabin. Close enough to watch Teddie?

Despite the warmth of the flames, he shivered. Was that where the guy was now?

Nobody sat around the campfire. On the other side of it, a sleeping bag was rolled up next to a knocked-over tent. Had the person been setting up camp or taking it down?

And where the hell was he now?

Manny blinked several times, trying to clear his vision. But the smoke was making it worse. Instead of moving away from the fire, though, he moved closer, circling around it to investigate the sleeping bag and the tent.

Maybe there was a backpack lying there, too. Or at least something that would give him a clue to the camper's identity. But as Manny stepped closer, he found the only thing that lay atop the collapsed tent was a ski mask—just as she'd described her attacker as wearing.

It wasn't cold enough for the camper to need the mask for warmth. No. This was the camp of the man who had attacked Teddie. So he must have started the fire. He intended to come back, then.

Should Manny wait for him to return?

Nerves of uneasiness moved through his gut. He was more concerned about where the hell the guy was now than if he would come back here. Had he returned to the cabin?

Was he going to try to attack Teddie again?

Manny had had to carry her into the cabin, she'd been so exhausted from her earlier struggle with her attacker. He doubted she would be able to fight off the stalker a second time.

"Son of a bitch." He cursed himself this time. Manny should not have left her. He needed to get back to her as soon as possible if he could even figure out which direction the damn cabin was in.

The smoke shifted, then began to take the form of a dark shadow. Before Manny could point his gun, the shadow raised a huge stick and swung it toward Manny's head.

He ducked that blow but braced himself for the next as the shadow swung again. He was determined to strike Manny, determined to take him out. And Manny wasn't certain he could see well enough to fight him off.

Chapter 4

"I can fly out in this," Cole insisted, glancing out of the hangar into the nearly impenetrable fog that surrounded the old metal structure. He had flown in far worse weather conditions with enemies trying to shoot him down. "Lend me your plane."

The older man snorted and shook his head. "Lots of dead pilots thought they could fly out in fog like this. They never made it wherever they'd intended to go."

"I have to get to the UP," Cole said. And those dead pilots hadn't been him.

"And you want to crash my plane doing it?" Walt asked him. He didn't know the old crop duster's last name, just his first. "Where's your little Cessna? You already crash it?"

"I lent it to a friend," Cole said. "And now he needs my help." That was what it had sounded like when

Cooper had called him earlier. Someone had attacked the client, and Manny had disappeared while trying to track down the assailant.

Letting Manny go alone to the UP had been a serious mistake. Sure, the whole thing had seemed funny at first. Manny thinking he was protecting a man only to find a gorgeous supermodel instead had seemed like the ultimate prank, like the ones they used to play on each other in boot camp.

It would have been hilarious. Except for the whole dangerous stalker part of the scenario. There was nothing funny about that.

"Come on, Walt," Cole pleaded, and he reached for his wallet. "I need that plane. How much will you take for it?"

Walt snickered. He probably didn't think Cole could actually afford it. But then, Walt had seen his new Cessna, since they kept theirs in the same hangar, so he had to know that Cole could pay him what his old crop duster was worth and then some. "Money's not the most important thing to everyone, son."

It was to Cole's family. They would kill each other over it if they thought they could get away with murder. And given how much money they had, they probably could.

"I'm sure your friend would rather have you alive than risking your life for him," Walt said.

Knowing Manny as well as he did, Cole had to agree. Manny wouldn't want him risking his life or even spending money on him. Manny was one of the few people Cole knew to whom money was not the most important thing. That was why he was such a good friend. Except for the other guys from their unit, Cole didn't have many people like Manny in his life. That was why he couldn't lose him.

"His life is in danger," Cole said. "I need to get there." He glanced out the open doors and shivered slightly as he noticed the fog had thickened even more.

Walt had moved away from the table where he'd been sitting. He squeezed Cole's arm now. "And risking your life isn't going to save his."

Cole could have argued. He had examples. The missions they'd survived because they'd done exactly that, risked their lives for each other. "Walt..."

Walt squeezed harder. "Once the fog lifts, you can borrow the plane," he said. "And all you need to do is fill the fuel tanks for me."

But Cole suspected it would be too late for him to help Manny once the fog lifted. Hell, he suspected it was already too late.

Cooper Payne had told her to stay in the cabin. But with every second that ticked by, it became harder and harder for Teddie to do *nothing*.

Jordan Mannes was out there alone, half-blinded *because of her*. His life was in danger *because of her*.

Of course, he was a bodyguard, so his life was probably often in danger. And she had hired his agency to protect her. But she was the one who had blinded him, making it more difficult for him to do his job: to protect her and to protect himself right now.

She should at least try to help him. But how? She had dropped the pepper-spray canister outside. It was probably empty anyway, though. And really, if a guy as big as her Payne Protection bodyguard hadn't been able to fight off her stalker, what would she be able to do?

The self-defense class she'd taken had taught her only the basics. She wasn't trained in hand-to-hand combat like Jordan Mannes undoubtedly was. How did one qualify to be a bodyguard? What was his background?

Why was she so curious about him? Teddie hadn't been curious about any man—but her stalker—in a long time. And all she'd wondered about him was who the hell he was and why he wanted to terrorize her.

Jordan Mannes had saved her from the stalker. So of course she would be curious about the bodyguard and about the kind of man who risked his life for others like he regularly did. She'd not known many heroic men in her life. Her own father had abandoned her before she'd even been born.

Maybe Jordan wasn't as heroic as she'd thought. Maybe he had abandoned her, too. She could hardly blame him if he had after she'd pepper-sprayed him. But she'd heard no motor start up when he'd walked outside. Wherever he'd gone, he'd gone on foot. So he couldn't be that far...

Could he?

Teddie paced the small confines of the cabin, walking back and forth across the living room with her heart pounding fast and hard as if she was outside running again. She ventured closer to the window, stuck her fingers between the slats of the blinds and peered out. She could see nothing outside. It was as if the darkness had wrapped itself around the little cabin like a thick blanket.

She shivered. Even though it was just early autumn, the temperatures dropped a lot at night in the Upper Peninsula. But it wasn't the cold that had chilled her. It was that feeling she'd had—the one she'd gotten earlier in the woods—that she was suddenly not alone.

And then she heard it. The scrape of metal moving against metal.

Where was the noise coming from?

She tilted her head and listened intently, trying to identify the sound. What was making it? Or, more important, who was making it?

She peered intently around the cabin, searching the shadows. Jordan had said he'd searched it before rushing outside to rescue her.

So nobody could be inside.

And she had locked the door just like he'd told her to. But just to be safe, she headed toward the door to double-check. As she did, she saw the knob move, and now she knew that the scraping noise was the sound of a key sliding into the lock and turning it.

Someone was coming inside the cabin.

Her heart slammed against her ribs as fear overwhelmed her again.

When Jordan had told her he'd found the door unlocked, she'd known she had locked it. Somehow her stalker had gotten a key. And now he was about to get her.

The cabin was so small that there was no place for her to hide. It was also so small that if she tried to run out the patio door to the deck—which was the only other exit—he would see her for certain. He had already outrun her once; she knew that he would again, especially now that the muscles in her legs had cramped up. It took an effort for her to run just to the kitchen.

Even if he was too big for her to overpower, she had to try. She was not going down without one hell of a fight. She jerked open a kitchen drawer and grabbed the handle of the biggest knife in the utensil divider.

With it firmly clasped in her hand, she moved toward the electrical panel hidden behind one of the cabinet doors. And she threw the switch that shut off all of the power, plunging the cabin into darkness as complete as the darkness outside.

At least this way she had the element of surprise on her side. Maybe—just maybe—she could hurt him before he could hurt her.

She shivered as she waited for the attack. But this time she would not be the one getting attacked. She was going to be the attacker.

Manny cursed at the darkness. He'd almost gotten used to it outside. But the lights of the cabin had guided him back to her—after he'd chased off the stalker. He had dodged the guy's second swing and jerked the tree limb from his grasp. Then Manny had turned the gun toward the man, but before he had been able to fire, the stalker had slipped back into the darkness outside the circle of light the campfire cast.

But it wasn't just dark now. The air had turned so thick it was like quicksand, sucking him deeper and deeper. Fog had rolled in along with the night, getting thicker as the night grew later. He didn't know how late it was or how long he'd been gone.

Too long.

He had left Teddie Plummer alone for far too long.

What if the stalker had circled back after Manny had run him off from the campsite? He obviously knew these woods better than Manny did. He had hurried back as fast as he had been able to move through the trees—toward the lights he had barely been able to discern through that thick blanket of fog and night. But was he too late?

He fumbled with the keys he'd found on the ground shortly after the stalker had run off. The guy must have dropped them when he'd picked up the stick he'd swung at Manny. He tried them all until he found the one that unlocked the door. But just as he was about to push open the door, the lights went off inside the cabin.

He glanced around outside. Was the stalker out there? Had he cut the power line? Or had nature caused the outage?

This wasn't a storm, though—just fog. Hell, maybe it wasn't even that. Maybe it was his damn eyes blurring everything around him. They burned yet, tears streaming from them.

He needed to wash out the pepper spray completely.

But more than anything, he needed to make sure Teddie was safe. He opened his mouth to call out to her. But what if the stalker had slipped around him and headed back to the cabin?

What if he was already inside with Teddie?

It was better that Manny enter as quietly as he could. And despite his size, he was good at being quiet since his and his friends' lives had so often depended on being as silent and invisible as they could during their missions.

He worried that his and Teddie's lives depended on it now. He pushed the door open just wide enough for him to slip inside—not that much light could spill into the house from the outside or from the inside out.

It was too damn dark.

He hunched over as he moved through the cabin, trying to make himself a smaller target. Whoever was inside had had time to get used to the darkness—while his irritated eyes were still trying to adjust. Maybe it wasn't that dark, though; maybe he was just blind.

His knee bumped against something soft. It must have been the couch. The tiny kitchen was situated behind the living area, so he turned. And just as he turned, he noticed a glint of something in the darkness.

He recognized the blade of a knife as it swung toward him. He didn't want to fire his gun in the dark, but he swung it toward that blade. Metal clinked against metal. Using the barrel of his gun to hold off the blade, he propelled his body forward—into the body of the person armed with the knife.

The damn stalker would not get away from him this time. And if the man had already hurt Teddie…

Where the hell was she? Tied up in the darkness? Or worse, already dead?

When he settled his body onto the body of the person he had knocked to the floor, he realized where Teddie was—lying beneath him. Her soft curves cushioned his muscles. And he was struck dumb for a moment at the intimate contact between their bodies. Her hips cradled his, her legs tangled with his, and her soft breasts yielded to the hardness of his chest. The contact set off a reaction inside him.

Adrenaline had already been coursing through him from his earlier encounters with the stalker and with her, but another kind of adrenaline entirely gripped him now. His pulse raced, his heart pounded and his mouth had gone so dry he couldn't speak.

The guys would laugh if he ever admitted that. They wouldn't believe that Manny Mannes had ever been speechless. Hell, he couldn't believe it, either.

Teddie squirmed and struggled beneath him and tried to swing the knife at him again. He dropped his gun and instinctively grabbed her wrist, closing his fingers around the delicate flesh.

He could feel the fear and the desperation in her, and he could hear it when she released a scream like the one that had first drawn him from the cabin and into the darkness.

"Shh," he said, finally finding his voice, which sounded strained even to his ears. "It's me. Jordan Mannes." He cleared his throat. "It's just me…"

Her body went limp beneath his as her breath escaped in a gasp that warmed his skin. She dropped the knife, then threw her arms around his neck. Pulling him close, she arched against him, molding their bodies even more intimately together.

"Oh, thank God, thank God," she murmured, "you're all right."

He wasn't all right, though. He was the furthest thing from all right that he had ever been. And it wasn't because his eyes still streamed from the pepper spray or he'd been attacked by her stalker and now by her…

He wasn't all right because his body was reacting to her. Every muscle was taut, and he had an intense ache in his groin. A tension gripped him that had nothing to do with the threat her stalker posed.

Manny was experiencing another kind of threat entirely. He was attracted to his client. And with a crazed stalker on the loose, that attraction was a distraction that neither of them could afford, not if they were going to survive the night.

He strongly suspected the stalker would come back to the cabin to try for her again. After she'd escaped him earlier that night, the man hadn't gone far away from her—just to his campsite.

He was determined.

And Manny's presence had seemed to do little to faze him. In fact, it might have made him even more intent on getting her. Manny had no backup. It was up to him to keep her safe. So he had to stay focused—to keep them both alive.

Chapter 5

Who the hell was that muscle-bound giant? And where had he come from?

Anger coursed through him, and he kicked one of the rocks around his fire pit, sending the stones into the flames, which flickered as sparks shot everywhere.

He jumped back, not wanting to get burned, not so soon after nearly being shot. The guy had a gun. He'd swung the barrel toward him, could have shot him if he hadn't moved faster.

Then he remembered the conversation he'd overheard as he'd crept around the house where Teddie had grown up, the house where her crazy mother had nearly shot him. Didn't she realize who he was?

That *he* was her daughter's destiny? Her soul mate? She was supposed to be with *him*. And only him…

But her mother, that crazy gun-wielding bitch, had

suggested that Teddie hire a bodyguard from the Payne Protection Agency.

Was that supposed to be some kind of joke? Nobody could protect anyone else from pain. He'd felt it his entire life, growing up with parents who'd never considered him good enough. And now he felt it every time Teddie ignored him and what they could have together.

Did she not think he was good enough for her, either?

How could she not see that they were perfect for each other? Why did she keep fighting him?

And now she had someone else to fight for her—another idiot with a gun, just like her crazy mother. Maybe *he* needed to get a weapon of his own. He wasn't certain how long it would take, but he would have no problem passing a background check. He had never done anything wrong to be refused the right to carry a weapon.

Even now he wasn't doing anything wrong.

He was just going to take what was his. *She* was *his* and his alone.

Even though he would pass, he couldn't wait for a background check to clear him to own a firearm. He would have to find another weapon to use to eliminate her bodyguard. He would not tolerate anyone trying to come between him and what was his. And if he couldn't have Teddie, well then, nobody would.

"I'm so sorry," Teddie said, blinking against the sudden light as Jordan flicked on the power again. She stared down at the knife lying on the hardwood floor next to his gun. She had nearly stabbed him. Well, maybe not *nearly*. He had disarmed her quickly and easily.

Jordan closed the cabinet of the electrical panel. "You have no reason to be sorry," he said.

Now she stared at him in shock. "I pepper-sprayed you," she reminded him.

Not that he would have needed the reminder. His eyes were still red, still watering.

"And I could have killed you." She gestured at the long knife.

He chuckled as he leaned over and picked up the knife and the gun. He slid the gun back into the holster he wore over his black T-shirt. The cotton was molded to his heavily muscled chest, and his arms bulged.

And she almost laughed, too, at the ridiculous notion that *she* could have hurt *him*. He held the knife, handle out, toward her.

But she shook her head. "I don't want it back."

"If you don't want to hang on to it, at least keep it close," he advised her. "You were smart to arm yourself. I should have told you I was at the door."

"You had a key," she said, and she tensed at the sudden realization. "I didn't give my keys to the Payne Protection Agency." So how was it that he had a set?

"I found them," he explained, "when I found your stalker's campsite in the woods."

She shivered, as she was thoroughly chilled again. For a little while, when she'd realized the intruder was her bodyguard, she had felt safe—especially in his strong arms, pressed against his hard body.

She had felt things other than safe, too. She'd felt an attraction, a need for closeness, that she hadn't experienced in a very long time and maybe never at that intensity.

But his words had completely shattered her brief sense of security.

"You found his campsite?" she asked as fear skittered throughout her again. "He's camped out close to here?"

Within sight? She felt as if he was always watching her—no matter where she was, no matter how far she'd gone to try to escape him.

Jordan Mannes's massively broad shoulders moved up and down as he shrugged. "I don't know how close the camp was. It was so damn dark out there, I got turned around. I couldn't tell you now exactly where it was."

She moved nearer to him and touched his face, which was almost as red as his eyes. His skin was burned from the spray, as well. Beneath her fingertips, it was warm and a little rough from the stubble of his beard.

"That's because of the pepper spray," she said. Her eyes had finally stopped burning, but that was because she'd washed her face after he'd left her alone in the cabin. "You need to get all of that off you."

She moved her hand along his hard jaw to his dark hair. She could see droplets glistening in it. Maybe he'd brought the fog inside with him, or maybe she had gotten the spray in his hair, too. "You need to shower it all off."

He shook his head and dislodged her hand. She curled her fingers against her palm. Her skin was tingling. Maybe it was from contacting the spray again or maybe it was from touching him.

"I have to keep watch," he said. "He got away from me."

"You saw him?" she asked.

"Not much of him," Jordan replied. "He tried hitting me over the head. Then he ran off. That was when he dropped the keys." He pulled a ring of keys from the pocket of his worn jeans.

She stared down at them, but they didn't look familiar to her. They didn't look like her set of keys, but then, a copy didn't have to look the same as long as the notches were identical. Her head began to pound as she tried to think of how that was possible. "I don't know how he would have gotten those."

"Have you given out any keys?"

She shook her head. "I don't give out keys." She had never had a relationship that had been serious enough to exchange keys. Except for one. "Only to my mom."

He stared down at her as if he was skeptical. He had probably read some of the tabloid articles about her. For years there had been a new one every week, claiming that she was involved with some actor or rock star.

"I hope you don't believe everything you've heard about me," she said.

He cocked his head as if searching his memory. Then he shrugged again. "What would I have heard?"

"Plenty of stuff that's not true," she assured him. She didn't date famous people. She didn't want to be famous herself. She had never wanted to be; she'd started modeling only to help out her mother.

"I've just been back in the States for a few months," he said. "So I'm not caught up on my celebrity gossip."

"I'm not a celebrity," she said, but then grimaced when she heard how sharp her voice sounded.

He snorted. "Yeah, right. I haven't been gone that long. It took me a little while to put it all together. But I know who you are."

Nobody really knew who she was. They only knew what she looked like.

She was sick of talking about herself. She was far more curious about him, and now she had an opportunity to satisfy her curiosity.

"Where were you," she asked, "that you've only been back a few months?"

"My Marine Corps unit was deployed," he said.

Marines. Of course. That was why he was so muscular. She knew male models who had spent thousands of dollars on personal trainers and performance products trying to achieve Jordan Mannes's impressive physique. They'd never come close to his masculine perfection.

Being a Marine would have definitely qualified him to be a bodyguard. She should have felt safer with him protecting her. But her interest—and attraction to him—unnerved her. She had never been so fascinated with anyone before.

But maybe she was just desperate for something to get her mind off her own life, off her stalker.

"Thank you," she said.

He arched a dark brow. "For what?"

"Your service." To their country and to her.

He nodded. But he didn't look comfortable with the gratitude. "Just doing my job."

She knew that being a Marine was much more than just a job. She wanted to talk to him more about his life.

But he reached for his weapon.

And she tensed. "What is it? Did you hear something?"

He shook his head. "No. So maybe now's a good time to take that shower you suggested." He squinted as his eyes continued to water. "Do you know how to shoot a gun?"

She shook her head.

He cocked it and handed it to her. "If someone tries to get in here, you squeeze the trigger." He wrapped most of her fingers around the handle while he stretched one finger along the barrel. "You'll need both hands to hold it."

It was cold and heavy. And she was terrified of accidentally firing it.

"Move this finger to the trigger if you hear anything," he advised.

"But…"

"He knows I'm armed," Manny said. "I nearly shot him. So I don't think he would be stupid enough to burst in here. But I want you to be ready in case he does."

He walked over to the hallway leading to the door, his broad back toward her.

And afraid of shooting him, Teddie lowered the barrel. "Why are you trusting me with this?" she asked. "Didn't I nearly kill you enough times already?"

He chuckled as he locked the front door and picked up a backpack she hadn't noticed sitting next to it. "Good thing for me that *nearly*s don't count," he said. "Or I would have been dead a hell of a long time ago."

She wondered about that, about how dangerous his life was, after he closed the bathroom door. When the

shower started, she wondered about something else—
how he looked standing naked under the spray of water.

Her hands began to shake, and it wasn't just from
the weight of the weapon she held. It was because her
pulse had begun to race again. The stalker wasn't the
only danger she faced.

She was in danger of becoming entirely too enthralled with her bodyguard. But just as she had never
wanted to date famous people, she wouldn't want to
date anyone like him. She wanted a simple life in which
she knew her husband would return home to her every
night.

She didn't need another man abandoning her like
her father had. Of course, that had been his choice—
to never be involved in hers and her mother's lives.
Once he'd gotten what he wanted from her mom, he'd
dropped the girl he hadn't considered good enough for
the school's star athlete.

It probably wouldn't be Jordan Mannes's choice to
abandon his family. With his dangerous life, he would
just eventually run out of *nearly*s.

The cold shower had washed away the pepper spray,
but it hadn't washed away the attraction Manny felt for
his client. The goose bumps had left his chilled skin
the minute he'd opened the bathroom door and found
her standing with the gun in her hands, trained at that
back door, as if she was protecting him.

Her arms and hands had been trembling as he'd
taken the weapon from her. He wondered if she'd even
blinked or had stared, wide-eyed, at the door the entire
time he'd been in the shower.

"It's okay," he told her. "He didn't come back."

Yet. But they both knew he would. The disturbed guy who'd sent her all of those threatening notes was obviously obsessed with her.

At the moment Manny could relate. She was something else. And it wasn't just her beautiful face and goddess-like body. It was her spirit.

She had a fire inside her that matched the color of her long, curly hair. He could just imagine releasing all that passion…

But imagine was all he could do. She was a client. Even if she wasn't, she would be off-limits to a guy like Manny. Despite her assertion that she wasn't, Teddie Plummer damn well was a celebrity. He was just a bodyguard, the person the paparazzi never even noticed standing next to the celebrity. Usually the celebrity didn't notice them, either. Teddie probably wouldn't have if there were more than just the two of them in the cabin.

"I need to check in with my boss," he said as he realized he should have done that earlier. But he hadn't had much of a chance.

Her lips parted on a gasp. "I called him," she confessed, "when you didn't come back right away."

He groaned. Cooper was probably furious with him. Manny had handled nothing about this assignment correctly. He was unlikely to ever get another solo one even if he actually managed to survive this one.

"I was worried," she said.

About herself or him?

"I thought something happened to you."

And his heart shifted. Was she a celebrity? Since they'd met she certainly hadn't acted like one. Not that he had any firsthand knowledge of how a celebrity actually acted. He could only go by what the media portrayed, and even vacuous reality stars acted more entitled and spoiled than this successful supermodel.

"I'm glad you called him," Manny said even though he had to brace himself as he pulled out his cell phone. The screen was black, though. No wonder Cooper hadn't tried to call him back. The phone was dead.

Teddie glanced down at the black screen. "That happens up here," she said. "Trying to get a signal drains the battery." She picked up a phone from the small kitchen counter. "I researched what carrier gets the best service up here, so use mine." She held it out to him.

He had learned to never rush off unprepared again. Hopefully his boss wouldn't think he'd learned that lesson too late.

"Thanks," he said. As he took it from her fingers, her skin flushed.

Or maybe it had already been red. She had gotten some of the pepper spray on herself.

"Do you need to shower?" he asked her. "Get that stuff off you, too?"

She lifted a hand to her face. "I—I washed it off already."

But her thick hair looked dry. "You showered?"

She shook her head. "No. I probably should."

As she headed toward the bathroom, he swallowed a groan. That had been a mistake, suggesting she get naked. He had already been having a hard enough time not imagining her that way.

Forcing his mind back on task, he punched the redial button to call the last number.

"Ms. Plummer," Cooper responded immediately. "Has Mannes returned yet?"

"Yeah, he has," Manny answered.

He heard Cooper's muttered but heartfelt "Thank God" before his "What the hell were you thinking going off and leaving her alone?"

"I was thinking I could catch the sick bastard and wrap up this assignment right away," Manny said.

"So did you?"

He sighed. "No. The son of a bitch got away from me."

Cooper must have heard the frustration in his voice because he didn't berate him. Manny was berating himself, though. He should have just shot the creep, but he would have been lucky to hit him with his blurry vision.

"You okay?" Cooper asked with concern.

Manny shrugged it off. He didn't deserve it. He had been a fool to leave her alone.

"Yeah," he replied. "I'm okay."

"She told me that she mistook you for her stalker and sprayed you."

"I'm fine now," Manny assured him. "I'll be able to fly us back to River City soon."

"Not tonight," Cooper said.

"My eyes are fine now," he said. They weren't, though. They were sore. But at least he could see.

"The airports are all closed down here," Cooper said. "Too much fog."

Manny cursed as he moved to the window and peered through the slats of the blinds. The fog was even thicker here now, too, wrapping tightly around the cabin. "Yeah, it's foggy here, too."

"Can you secure where you're at?" Cooper asked him. "Then I'll get reinforcements up to you as soon as possible."

"If I can't fly into River City, then nobody can get out of it," Manny pointed out. As he peered through the slats of the blinds, he doubted anybody could see in this fog, either, even if he hadn't been maced. "I don't think even Cole could fly in this."

And Cole was a better pilot than he was. He'd been flying longer.

Cooper snorted. "He's trying."

Manny cursed. "Don't let him! It's not worth the risk. I scared the stalker away. He thought she was alone up here. That's why he tried for her earlier. Now that he knows she has a bodyguard, I'm sure he'll back off." He was only saying that so his friends wouldn't worry. Manny didn't believe a word he spoke. And as he stared out the window, he noticed a shift in the darkness, as if something—or someone—was moving around out there.

Just as he'd suspected, the son of a bitch wasn't giving up on getting to Teddie. But he would have to go through Manny to do that.

Chapter 6

"He's out there, isn't he?" Teddie asked her body-guard as Jordan Mannes peered through the blinds.

He didn't have to nod to confirm her fears. She always knew when *he* was watching her. She could feel it like a chill rushing over her skin.

She shivered. Maybe she shouldn't have taken that shower an hour ago. While it had washed away the last vestiges of the pepper spray, it had done nothing to warm her. Her hair was so thick that the blow-dryer could never completely dry it. It hung down her back, dampening her sweatshirt. She shivered again.

"He knows I'm armed," Jordan said. "So he knows better than to try anything."

"He's crazy," Teddie said as she picked up the folder from the small desk where she'd been sitting. She opened it to all those mutilated photos and threats. "Nothing he says or does makes any sense."

Mannes walked over to the desk. "I saw those when I first got here."

She gasped as she realized the photograph on the top was a new one. She recognized the scenery around the cabin, and she recognized herself—despite how mutilated the figure was—in the middle of that photo. It had been taken right here, and she knew when. Thinking she was safe, she had gone for a run the first day she'd settled into the cabin. The weather had been so warm that she'd been wearing shorts and a tank top. The top was gone, as was her face. Had she looked happy when the picture was taken?

She'd felt happy then. She shouldn't have. Obviously she didn't always know when he was watching her.

"This one's new," she said, and she pointed to it with a trembling fingertip. "It wasn't in here before."

"That must be why I found the door unlocked," Mannes said. "He let himself inside to leave that."

She glanced toward the door and shivered again. She had been foolish to think she would be safe anywhere from him.

"I have the keys now," Manny reminded her. "He can't just let himself inside again."

She doubted that not having a key would stop him. There were windows. The glass patio door. He could break any of those and get inside if he wanted to.

And he obviously wanted to.

"Who is he?" Mannes asked.

She glanced up at him. "You think I know?"

"You must have some idea," he said. "An ex-boyfriend? Jilted lover?"

She shook her head. "No."

She couldn't believe that anyone she had trusted

enough to date could have done this. Well aware of her mother's heartbreak, Teddie was always very choosy about whom she dated. That was why she rarely dated.

If only she'd been as careful with some of the friends she'd made…

"No way," she said. "It has to just be some obsessed fan. One of those guys who bought all the posters…"

A muscle moved along his jaw, as if he was flinching. And he shook his head. "These photos don't look like posters. They're all candid shots—especially this one."

Teddie flinched now. "You'd be surprised how many candid shots have been sold to tabloids," she remarked with bitterness. "I can't go to a friend's house to swim without one of them selling the picture they snapped without me even realizing it. I even had one hide a camera in her changing room to get a picture of me naked."

She remembered how devastated she'd been when she had found the camera. Thankfully she had found it before she'd even taken off her clothes. Because once those photos got out there, they were out.

"Those aren't friends," Mannes said. "They're opportunists. Could one of them…?" He gestured at the pictures.

She shook her head. "They're opportunists," she agreed. "They aren't sick."

Mannes sighed. "I can't imagine not having the friends I do—guys I can trust." His brow furrowed slightly. "Well, guys I can trust most of the time."

Teddie sighed, too. "I can't trust anyone," she said, "ever."

"Yes, you can," he said.

She glanced up at him. "You?"

"Yes," he said. "But you've just met me, so I don't expect you to believe that."

A smile tugging at her lips, she said, "That's good." Because she would find it very hard to trust a man like Jordan Mannes. Sure, he seemed dedicated to his job. But a job and a woman were very different.

"I was talking about your mother," he added.

"Yes, I trust my mother," she said. "Or I wouldn't have called the Payne Protection Agency at all. Hiring you was her idea."

"Your mother sounds like a smart woman," he said.

"She is." Although her mom didn't believe that herself. Because she'd dropped out of school when she'd gotten pregnant with Teddie, she thought she was stupid and inferior. That was probably what Teddie's father had told her, too. Her mother had no idea how smart she was. Or strong.

Teddie wished she was half the woman her mother was. That was why she worked so hard—to make her mother proud. That was also why she was so careful about whom she dated.

"She would love you," she said, surprising herself that she had admitted it aloud. But Mama *would* love him, especially how protective he was.

"I'm not so sure about that," he said. "I'm usually not a big hit with moms."

She studied him for a moment. "So maybe I shouldn't trust you."

"You're paying Payne Protection to protect you," he said. "You can trust me."

"I couldn't trust other people I paid," she said. "Former agents, former assistants, former friends…" She forced a laugh. "God, I sound pathetic—having my own little pity party here."

"You're entitled," he said. "Even though you don't act like it."

She frowned, uncertain of what he meant. But other people had said that to her, as well. That she was down-to-earth. She couldn't come from where she had and not be down-to-earth, though.

"Could your stalker be one of them?" he asked. "A former agent or assistant or friend?"

She shook her head. "I don't believe that. Nobody who ever worked for me or with me was ever obsessed with me." And whoever had sent those sick photos clearly was.

Jordan closed the folder. "We'll get this back to Payne Protection," he said. "One of my fellow body-guards is an ace at tracking stuff down online. She can figure out where all these photos were taken." He held up the picture shot outside the back door. "This one will be easy enough. But by tracking down all the other ones, as well, she might also be able to figure out who could have taken them."

Teddie wasn't certain how that would be possible. She suspected the photos came from multiple sources. The ones he hadn't taken himself, her stalker had prob-ably found online.

"We will figure this out," he assured her.

She studied his handsome face for a moment. He was so strong but also smart. "I thought you were just a bodyguard."

He shrugged those broad shoulders. "Best way to protect someone is to identify and eliminate the threat."

"Are you talking about being a bodyguard or a Marine?"

"The job is very similar," he said as he moved back to the window and peered through the blinds, "which is probably why so many bodyguards are former Marines."

It made sense, and lately not much else had made sense to Teddie. She didn't even make sense to herself anymore.

Why was she so attracted to this stranger?

She had met far more handsome men. It must be the hero thing. He'd rescued her. He'd protected her. Was this just gratitude she felt for him?

It had to be. They had nothing else in common. She couldn't get involved with someone she couldn't trust. And with a job as dangerous as his, he couldn't be trusted to stick around.

Maybe he had only imagined that movement in the dark earlier, because Manny could see nothing moving around outside now. Or maybe that was because the fog had thickened even more—which made it pointless for him to keep looking out the windows.

And yet it was safer than looking at *her*.

She was every bit the distraction he'd been afraid she would be. She was so damn beautiful, even without makeup. Her hair hung in damp tendrils around her shoulders, and baggy sweats enveloped her body. But yet she was drop-dead gorgeous.

He almost couldn't blame her stalker. But he did—for terrifying her. And he wanted to hurt the man because of what he was putting her through. That was why he kept looking out the window. He wanted the creep to show himself again now that his vision was clear and he could get a good look at him. Or a good shot at him.

He'd been trained as a sniper in the Marines. He was a damn good shot when he could see. But while the pepper spray no longer had his eyes burning, the fog blinded him to whoever might be lurking around the cabin. He wasn't able to see the stalker, but Manny instinctively knew he was out there.

Unfortunately, so did she. Teddie was obviously and rightfully unnerved. The guy had grabbed her once that night. She had every right to worry that he would try again.

To get her mind off her stalker, he gestured toward the textbooks. "What are those about? Are you a professor?"

She laughed. "I wish."

"Really?" He couldn't see her hanging out in the stuffy halls of academia. Actually, he could imagine her dressed as a sexy professor, chewing on the earpiece of her black glasses as she unbuttoned her sweater. That had been a bra advertisement featuring her. Unfortunately, he remembered it too well and his blood started to pump hot and fast through his veins, all rushing to one part of his body.

"I don't really want to be a professor," she said. "But I've been taking college classes since I got my GED."

"GED?"

"My mother didn't want me to drop out of high school to model," she said. "I was just fifteen when I won a contest to represent a suntan-lotion company. So I talked Mama into letting me accept the contract if I was able to pass the test and get my GED." She smiled. "I passed."

"You started modeling young, then," he said, even though he knew that she had. He didn't want to admit how long he'd admired her photographs.

She nodded. "You have to start young in this business."

"So your mom was fine with you going off to model suntan lotion at fifteen as long as you had your GED?" he asked.

"What about you?" she asked, her beautiful face tensing as she got defensive. "Was your mother fine with you going off to join the Marines?"

"I was eighteen," he said. "And she was glad to get rid of me. From the way you talk about your mom, you two seem closer than me and my mom." His mom really had been happy he'd joined the Marines, though. She'd preferred he go there rather than prison.

"We didn't have much choice," she said. "We needed the money, or we would have lost our house."

"What about your dad?" He couldn't imagine a father being okay with his daughter modeling swimsuits and lingerie.

She shrugged. "I have no idea," she said. "I've never met him. It's always been just me and my mom."

That was probably why Teddie spoke so fondly of her mother. Most of his life it had been just him and his mom, but he doubted she spoke as fondly of him.

"She was seventeen when she had me," Teddie added. "She never graduated from high school. That's why it was so important to her that I get my diploma. And now I'm going for my bachelor's degree."

"You're going to college right now?" he asked.

"I'm just taking online classes," she said. "Too many people recognized me when I tried to attend an actual class on campus."

He doubted she could go anywhere without being recognized. "Is that why you came up here?" he asked. And he probably sounded like one of those reporters who always hounded her when he fired more questions at her. "To study? Or to get away from people recognizing you?"

"Both," she admitted.

"So, what are you going to do with your degree?" he asked. As successful as she had been in modeling, he doubted she needed more money—unless she'd already blown it all.

"I want to teach little kids," she said. "Like kindergarten or first grade."

That was a shock. He'd figured she'd want to do something within the industry she knew, like become an agent herself or a fashion designer. Maybe she really did want to get completely out of the business.

"You don't think *they'll* recognize you?" he asked about the kids.

"I'm no Disney princess," she said with a smile, "so, no, I don't think they will."

"Is this because of him?" he asked. "Are you letting the stalker make you change your whole lifestyle?"

She shuddered. "Not at all. I was getting ready to retire even before he sent that first letter. If anything, I stayed longer out of pride, to prove to myself and to him that he didn't scare me."

"Liar."

She gasped.

"You'd be a fool not to be afraid," he said. "And

you're no fool." In fact, she was damn impressive with all her textbooks and her goal of becoming a teacher.

She shook her head, tumbling the damp red tendrils around her shoulders. "I wish that were true. But I was a fool to trust the people I trusted."

"We all make mistakes." But one of her mistakes might have betrayed her even more than she wanted to believe. Maybe when one of her former friends had no longer been able to take and sell photos of her, he had begun to desecrate them.

"I'm going to be very careful from now on," she said. "I want nothing to do with fame and fortune. I just want to have a nice quiet life where nobody wants to take my picture or publish some garbage about me."

Despite her protests, Manny worried that she had let the stalker's threats affect her. Once he—and Payne Protection—caught and stopped the guy, she would be able to decide what she really wanted out of life.

Maybe it was the peace and quiet—maybe it was the fame. Anyway, it wouldn't affect Manny. There was no place in either version of her life for a guy like him. He wouldn't fit in with her in the spotlight or in the quiet life.

"Manny's fine," Cooper assured his team as he joined them in the airplane hangar where Cole had gone to wait out the fog. Sometime during the night the others had joined him. Dane, Lars and Cooper's sister Nikki played cards with an old guy while guzzling coffee.

He wrinkled his nose at the smell of coffee burning to sludge in the bottom of the pot on the back burner.

Cole leaped to his feet, his blue eyes dark with anxiety. "You heard from him? We've all been trying his phone, but it keeps going straight to voice mail."

"It's dead," Cooper said.

Nikki nodded. "Our wireless carrier probably doesn't have a good signal in the UP, so it drained his battery."

"He called me from her phone," Cooper said. "And he was all right. He's just frustrated that he almost had the guy but lost him in the woods."

Lars chuckled. "Manny in the woods? I'm surprised he didn't get lost."

Cooper suspected that he might have. But of course it hadn't helped that he had been pepper-sprayed. He couldn't believe he'd gone after the stalker in such a compromised condition. But Manny was tough.

"He might have gotten lost. That was probably why he was so pissed," Cooper allowed.

Dane chuckled, too. "That sounds like Manny. He's more likely to get pissed off at himself than someone else."

Actually, he hadn't sounded like Manny, though. Despite how good a Marine and a bodyguard Jordan Mannes had always been, he had never sounded as determined and focused and pissed off as he had during their conversation. And Cooper thought he hadn't been mad just at himself. He'd wanted to catch that stalker; he'd wanted to stop him.

"So, how badly did he yell at you for messing with him?" Lars asked.

Cooper shook his head. "He didn't."

And Cooper wouldn't have blamed him if he had. He had it coming. As the boss, he should have made certain his employee was aware of the situation into which he was walking. But he'd trusted Manny to jump right in and handle the challenges. And of course, he had. He'd saved the client.

Cole was still all nervous energy. He strode past Cooper to the open hangar door. Peering out, he said, "It's starting to clear."

The fog was as thick as ever. Cooper had had to roll down his window and peer out the side of his SUV to see on the drive to the private airstrip.

"We should be able to leave soon," Cole persisted, his lean body tense with anxiety.

"I just told you that he's fine," Cooper assured Manny's best friend.

But as Manny's best friend, Cole clearly knew better. "No, he's not."

"He shouldn't be alone up there with no backup," Dane said as he joined them at the open hangar door. "That stalker's still on the loose."

"He's in danger," Cole insisted.

Cooper wasn't certain what threat Cole was worried about: the stalker or Teddie Plummer. He suspected they both posed a danger to Manny.

Chapter 7

Where was she?

Teddie jerked awake, blinking to clear her vision and focus on the room around her. She'd spent so many years traveling that she was used to waking up disoriented and unfamiliar with her surroundings.

She recognized the loft in the little A-frame cabin. And she was familiar with the bed on which she lay, the plaid flannel blankets pulled to her chin. She just didn't remember how she'd gotten there. Her last memory was of sitting on the couch, reading a physics textbook while her bodyguard had stood at the window, staring into the darkness.

She must have fallen asleep.

How had she gotten to her bed?

Had he carried her like he had up the back steps and into the house earlier? Had he tucked her into the bed?

Heat flashed through her body at the thought of being in his arms again. Had he undressed her, too?

She lifted the blankets to peek beneath them. No wonder she was hot; she was still wearing her sweatshirt and pants. She kicked off the blankets and stretched. She couldn't remember the last time she'd slept so soundly. Certainly not since the stalker had broken into Mama's house. Even before that, she'd awakened with nightmares—ever since that first threatening note.

Last night she had managed to sleep—deeply—thanks to her bodyguard. She, who struggled so hard to trust anyone, had instinctively trusted him to keep her safe.

Where was Jordan Mannes? Had he slept at all the night before or had he remained at that window the entire time, standing guard over her?

She rolled out of bed and peered over the loft rail to the living room below. There were no blankets on the couch, just her abandoned textbook. He hadn't slept there or he would have moved the book.

But he no longer stood at the window that glowed with the sun rising behind the blinds. Was he in the kitchen? She sniffed but could smell no scent of coffee or food. And her stomach rumbled as she realized how long it had been since she'd eaten. She had never been the kind of model who starved herself.

Growing up with a great cook like Mama, Teddie loved food too much to deny herself. And fortunately for her, a lot of designers had begun to appreciate the figures of real women. This real woman needed some food. But first she needed to know where her bodyguard had gone.

She hurried down the steep steps from the loft. Then

she heard it—the deep rumble of male voices. Not just his. There was another voice, as well.

Her heart slammed against her ribs. Had he caught the stalker? Was he talking to him?

The voices weren't raised in anger. Sometimes it was scarier when a man lowered his voice than raised it. She'd almost always preferred the photographers and ad execs who'd yelled to get what they wanted. The ones who'd spoken so coldly had intimidated her the most.

She moved closer to the door, trying to listen in on the conversation. But as she neared it, the door opened and she found not just Jordan's dark-eyed gaze trained on her but also another man staring at her. He was not as big as Jordan Mannes, but like him, he carried a gun.

She gasped and stepped back. Maybe she was not awake. Maybe she was still dreaming and this was her nightmare and her stalker.

Cole quickly holstered the weapon he'd instinctively drawn when he'd noticed the shadow beneath the back door. But the client continued to stare at him, her green eyes wide with fear. "It's okay," he assured her.

Manny didn't speak at all. He just stared at her like she was staring at Cole—with almost as much fear. That was what Cole had suspected, that she'd already started getting to Manny, or he would have demanded last night that Cooper pull him from the assignment.

He probably should have demanded that.

Nikki Payne pushed him and Manny aside and said, "Like Manny, we're with Payne Protection." She held out her hand. "I'm Nikki Payne. This is Cole Bentler.

My fiancé, Lars, and his bestie, Dane, flew up with us, too, but they're out searching the woods right now."

"Manny?" The redhead repeated the name, her brow furrowing with confusion.

Nikki glanced back at Manny. "Jordan Mannes— everybody calls him Manny."

Obviously the redhead had not been aware of that. Usually Manny shared his nickname with everyone. Had he been trying to keep things more formal—more professional—between them? That had probably been a good idea.

"Are you all right?" Nikki asked the question of Teddie Plummer. But Cole wanted to ask Manny, who had still not spoken. He couldn't remember his garrulous friend ever staying quiet for so long.

Teddie nodded. "Yes. I'm sorry. I'm—I'm a little disoriented. I just woke up and haven't had my coffee yet."

"I'll make some," Nikki offered as she followed the supermodel into the cabin.

Cole pulled the door closed behind the women and remained standing outside with his best friend. "Looks like you could use some coffee, too."

Manny ran a hand down over his face; it shook slightly. "Yeah, I could. I was up all night making sure he didn't try for her again."

"If he's out there, Lars and Dane will find him," Cole said.

Manny snorted. "Then who will find them? They're city boys like me. They're bound to get lost out there."

His getting lost had scared the hell out of the team the night before, especially Cole. But he'd be damned if he'd admit it. Such an admission would only embarrass them both. So he shrugged. "Nikki's probably planted a GPS locator on Lars like people do their pets."

Usually Manny would have been the one to make the joke about their friends being whipped. But he didn't even laugh.

"You really are tired," he said. "Why don't you go in the house and get some sleep?"

Manny shook his head. "I'm fine. It's not like I've never been sleep-deprived before."

"Yeah, when we were being tortured," Cole said. "That must be what this entire assignment is to you—torture."

Manny glanced at the closed door. Maybe he was worried that the client was going to overhear them. "It's fine. You can stop feeling guilty for going along with the joke."

Cole couldn't deny that he had been feeling guilty. His friend knew him too well. That went both ways, though. He knew Manny just as well. "I can take over as primary bodyguard for you," he offered.

Manny shook his head. "I told you it's fine."

"You said she maced you," Cole reminded him.

"Then she pulled a knife on me, too."

Cole had had the misfortune of knowing some dangerous women—some that he'd loved—but it sounded like Teddie Plummer could give them a run for their money. "What the hell—"

"That's what makes this such an easy assignment," Manny said. "She protects herself." He sounded impressed—maybe too impressed.

Cole was glad he had waited out the fog and flown out as soon as the weather had cleared. Because it was obvious—whether from the stalker or their beautiful client—that Manny needed protection.

Manny had been glad to see his friends—even though he'd pulled a gun on them the minute they'd arrived. Of course they'd expected it. He wouldn't have been doing his job if they had managed to sneak up on him.

The entire night he'd stayed alert to movement outside the cabin, to shadows shifting in the night and the fog. He'd also stayed alert to every sound Teddie had made as she murmured and shifted in her sleep.

His body was still tense, on edge with desire for her. God, she was beautiful. When he'd opened that door to see her glorious red hair tangled around her face and her features soft with sleep, he'd lost his mind for a moment. He hadn't been able to speak or even think or breathe.

He wanted her...

He wanted her to be safe. And the only way to do that would be to find the sick son of a bitch who was after her and destroy him.

Cole was talking to Manny as they stood outside the cabin. He didn't hear anything his friend was saying. Instead he heard the rustle of brush. And he drew his weapon, pointing it toward where he'd seen the brush rustle the night before. But the man emerging between the trees and underbrush was bigger than the one who had swung the stick at Manny near the campfire. Lars Ecklund was a blond giant of a man. And he was not alone. Dane Sutton walked out of the trees behind Lars.

"Well, they found their way back," Cole muttered

as he reholstered the gun he had drawn, as well. Then he called out to them. "Did you guys find anything?"

Lars sighed. "Probably just poison ivy."

Dane snorted but surreptitiously scratched at his arm despite wearing long sleeves. "We found an old campsite," he said. "Looks like the fire had been out for a while, though. The ashes of it were all that was left behind."

"He's gone," Lars said.

Manny shook his head. He knew he'd seen something outside that window—someone. "He's not far." Hell, he was probably watching them right now—if the skin prickling between Manny's shoulder blades was any indication. "I doubt he's ever very far away from her."

Dane glanced uneasily around the area, as if he felt it, too, that they were being watched.

"We need to bring her back to River City," Cole said, "and get her into one of the safe houses with around-the-clock protection, each of us taking a shift. You can't do this alone."

How bad did he look that his friend was so worried about him? Of course Cole was the worrier of the unit. He knew the worst that could happen. Probably because it had already happened to him.

"I don't intend to do this alone," Manny said. "I need your help to track down this guy. And it might be easier to do that here than in River City."

"How's that?" Nikki asked the question as she opened the door behind them.

"It's a remote area," he said with a faint shudder as he thought of all the woods around here and how easy it was to get lost in them. "So a stranger is going to stick out here. He's going to be memorable to the locals for buying his camping gear, for asking for directions to this place. He also got a set of keys to her place somehow."

Nikki stared at him in surprise. As he glanced around, he noticed the guys staring at him the same way, with their mouths just about gaping open with shock. They weren't the only ones. He had surprised himself, too. But he'd had the entire sleepless night to strategize how to catch this stalker. Otherwise he probably would have left it to everyone else, like he usually did.

He pulled the keys from his pocket and held them out to Nikki. "Teddie swears she hasn't given out any keys to anyone but her mother."

Nikki nodded. "Maybe he was there—when she had the keys made for her mom. Or he bribed a locksmith or something to come out and make a key for the lock." She studied the keys, her dark eyes narrowed. "We might be able to get prints off these, too."

"So you'll check the locksmith angle," Manny told her.

Then he turned toward Lars. "How about you check out the stores in town? See if any stranger bought some camping equipment lately?"

Then he turned to Dane. "Gas stations?"

But when he turned toward Cole, Bentler shook his head. "Nope," he said. "You're not sending me anywhere. I'm staying right here. You need backup."

"I'm alert," Manny said. There was no way he would be able to take the nap Cole had suggested. He was too wired, too close to catching this bastard to miss any opportunity. "And it's daylight. I'll see him coming if he's stupid enough to try again."

"He's right," Dane said. "The fog's burned off. It's easy to see now."

"You need to check at the airstrip," he told Cole, "see if anyone else has flown in recently. A stranger."

Cole sighed but nodded.

Nikki stepped closer to him and patted his cheek. She was so much like her mother—from the auburn curls to the warm brown eyes in appearance and the warmth and affection in personality. "Good work, Mannes," she said with approval. "Cooper was right to make you the lead bodyguard on this assignment."

"It was a joke," he reminded her. "Cooper was playing a joke on me." And everybody else had been in on it. He probably should have been furious with them, but they weren't like Teddie's friends. They hadn't sold him out for money or for fifteen minutes of fame. And they had his back when he needed it.

It also wasn't like he had never pulled a trick on any of them before. Sometimes kidding around was all that had gotten them through the tough missions. Actually, the tougher the mission, the more they had goofed around.

Nikki pulled a folder from the laptop bag strapped over her shoulder. "This is no joke," she said as she fanned through the stalker's sadistic threats. "Cooper wouldn't have sent you if he hadn't thought you could handle it."

Manny had thought he could handle whatever the assignment had entailed—before he'd learned the client was Teddie Plummer, the woman of his former fantasies. It wasn't just her distracting him that he had to worry about. He had to worry about her stalker, how sick and twisted and determined the man was to get to her.

Manny held on to the facade of confidence until they were all gone. But when he stepped into the cabin and found Teddie waiting for him, his doubts resurfaced. Oh, he knew he would find her stalker. He just wasn't certain what stopping the guy would cost him.

His life.

Or his heart…

Chapter 8

Hearing the engine as a vehicle pulled away had given Teddie a moment's panic that she had been left alone. Unprotected.

When the door opened and Jordan walked into the cabin, relief rushed over with such force that her knees nearly weakened. And she realized she hadn't been afraid of being left alone.

The Payne Protection Agency was too professional to leave her without a bodyguard. Her panic had been that she'd thought *he* had left her.

He must have seen her panic because he drew his weapon and peered around the cabin. "Are you all right?"

She jerked her head up and down in a quick nod, as emotion choked her. Maybe it had just all caught up with her—all the months of being watched, threatened, nearly grabbed...

Tears stung her eyes, but she blinked them back. She was not going to fall apart now. She was like her mama—tough. Drawing in a deep breath to calm herself, she nodded again. "Yes, I'm fine."

He holstered his weapon and reached for her, closing his arms around her. "You're not fine," he said as he drew her against his chest. "You're shaking."

Had the shock of the night before—of nearly being attacked—finally caught up with her? She was trembling, but she realized it had less to do with shock and more to do with being this close to Jordan Mannes. He was so big, so strong, so hard and warm.

She lifted her arms and linked them around his neck then tipped her head up toward his. She wasn't used to having to look up this much. At five-ten, she was nearly as tall if not taller than most of the men she met—except for him and his mammoth friends.

Only the female bodyguard had been small—petite even—but her personality had been larger than life. Despite the woman being a little younger than Teddie, Nikki Payne had reminded her of her mother. Shrewd and strong.

"Thank you for staying," she told him.

He tilted his head and his brow furrowed with confusion. "You thought I left?"

"I heard the engine start up," she said. "Then I heard the vehicle driving off."

"The others left," he told her, "but just for a little while. They're going to do some investigating. See if we can figure out who this guy is." While he kept one arm wrapped around her, he moved his other hand toward her face and ran his big fingers along her jaw. "And I'm not leaving you—not until this guy is caught."

But he would leave her then. She was just an assignment to him. She knew it was foolish to think otherwise. He was getting paid to protect her. She was paying him, just like she'd paid agents and assistants who had betrayed her.

Would Jordan Mannes betray her, too?

The night before she had been so vulnerable she had told him things that she'd shared with no one else—about the friends who'd betrayed her, about how she'd grown up with just her mom, about how she wanted to get her degree for her mama. Would she read those things in a tabloid someday?

She shuddered as she considered it.

"What's wrong?" he asked as he stared down into her face.

Other men rarely looked at her face. They stared instead at her oversize breasts and hips. They didn't bother looking into her eyes like Jordan was looking now. But she wondered if it was just her eyes into which he was looking or if it was her soul...

He seemed to see her in a way no one else had.

"I'm just scared," she said.

He drew her closer. "You can stop worrying," he told her. "I will protect you."

But at the moment it wasn't her stalker she was scared of; it was Jordan Mannes and the feelings he had rushing through her. Her pulse raced; her skin tingled. She wanted more than his protection.

She wanted him.

To close the distance between them, she only had to rise up on her toes. Then she pressed her mouth to his. His lips were cool and somehow both soft and hard beneath hers. And unmoving...

Embarrassed, she pulled back. "I'm sor—"

His mouth swallowed the rest of her apology as he kissed her back. His lips nipped and nibbled at hers until she opened her mouth. Then he deepened the kiss. Their breath mingled. He tasted fresh and minty. She probably tasted like coffee. He didn't seem to care.

His tongue slid over hers, teasing, stroking…

She wanted him to touch her like that other places, her breasts, her core…

But he held only her chin in one hand while he clutched the back of her sweatshirt in his other hand. He used her shirt to pull her away from him as he lifted his head away from hers. Then he dropped his hand from her face and rubbed it over his. "God, I'm sorry. I shouldn't have done that."

The apology stunned her for a moment. Then she reminded him, "I kissed you."

"But *I* shouldn't have crossed the line."

"And I should have?" she asked.

Did he really not believe everything he'd read about her? Or did he think she was the wild woman the tabloids had painted her to be?

"You're upset," he said. "You're vulnerable. I'm here to protect you—not take advantage of you. I shouldn't have touched you."

He had put his arms around her first—before she'd kissed him. But apparently he'd only been comforting her.

Her pride bristled. "I am not some weak damsel in distress."

"You don't have to tell me," he assured her. "You've maced me and pulled a knife on me."

And then she'd kissed him. No wonder he had been

taken aback. He probably thought she was losing her mind, especially since she'd misconstrued his comforting her as an invitation for her to kiss him. She groaned as embarrassment washed over her again.

"I'm the one who's sorry," she said. "I've just proved again that my judgment is impaired. I'm sorry—"

He pressed his fingers over her lips this time.

She would have preferred that he had pressed his mouth to hers. Her lips tingled from the contact with his skin, though. She could still taste him.

And she wanted more.

"Stop beating yourself up about this," he said. "That kiss had nothing to do with your judgment. I would know. I am an expert on bad judgment." He moved his fingers quickly away from her mouth, as if he considered touching her to be bad judgment.

"You?" she asked. "What mistakes have you made?"

He shook his head. "Not personally. I learned from the mistakes the other men in my family have made. My dad and brother are both in prison."

"Wow," she murmured. "That must be hard." And harder yet for him to escape that life and join the Marines.

He shrugged. "They made bad choices. First in women and then in the things they did to make those women happy." He shuddered. "That's why I have vowed to stay single. The Mannes men have very bad judgment when it comes to women."

Was he warning her off?

Her face heated as her embarrassment returned. She'd just kissed him. Not proposed. But she had wanted more than a kiss. She wanted more than that now.

"So since you're not in prison," he told her, "your judgment isn't that bad."

"Not bad enough to get me incarcerated," she agreed.

But if her stalker was someone she knew, it might have been bad enough to get her killed. Or if she fell for Jordan Mannes despite his warning, her bad judgment could get her heart broken.

Manny was an idiot. He should have let Cole take his place protecting her—because he had totally lost his objectivity. What the hell had he been thinking to kiss her?

Sure, she'd kissed him first—which had totally shocked him. Then he'd done the unforgivable. He'd kissed her. And he hadn't wanted to stop.

Her mouth was so hot, so sweet. He could have kissed her for hours. But he wouldn't have stopped there. He wouldn't have stopped at kissing—if he hadn't suddenly come to his senses and remembered that he had a job to do.

She was in danger, and he could not afford to be distracted. To clear his head, he stepped outside and was instantly blinded.

It wasn't pepper spray burning his eyes but the sudden flash of a camera bulb. Blinking and squinting, he swung out and knocked the camera to the ground.

"Hey!" the photographer shouted as he leaned over to reach for it—just as Manny kicked it. Along with a spray of gravel from the makeshift sidewalk, the camera flew several feet.

Then he reached for the guy. With his hand in his collar, he jerked him around to face him. "Who the hell are you?"

Was this the guy? The stalker? At around six foot, he was the right height. But he seemed skinnier than he had last night. And maybe a little older, his hair graying, to move as fast as he had through the woods.

The guy's pale face flushed with color and he stammered, "I—I'm a reporter."

"Where are your credentials?" he challenged the guy.

"I'm freelance."

Maybe a freelance stalker. He might not have been as old as he looked. Maybe he'd just gone prematurely gray.

Wanting to get to the truth, Manny pulled out the guy's wallet and flipped it open to a New York driver's license. "Bernard Setters." Behind the license, there was a press pass. That didn't necessarily mean it was legit, though.

"You know my name," the reporter said as if he expected Manny to recognize it—like he was somebody Manny should know. "Now tell me yours."

Manny snorted. He hadn't had a whole lot of experience with the media. The Corps had made sure the press had known nothing of their missions, and Cooper had handled all the reporters' questions after the assignments Manny had worked for the Payne Protection Agency. But he didn't need experience to know to reveal as little as possible.

His friends all thought he talked too much. But that was just to them—because he could trust them. He knew to never trust a reporter.

"You're trespassing," Manny told him. "You need to leave this property right now."

"You don't own this property," Setters told him.

"Teddie Plummer owns this property. I'm here to speak to her."

Manny doubted Teddie had put her own name on the deed since county websites were so easy to search for the names of property owners. This guy was probably just fishing.

"You must have been given misinformation," Manny told him. "No Plummer here. Let me escort you back to your vehicle." He gave the guy a little shove toward the hatchback parked in the driveway.

Just because he'd driven up didn't mean he wasn't the one who'd camped out around the house the night before, though. His hand grasping the back of this guy's leather jacket, Manny tugged him toward the car. As he neared it, he could see in the back. There was no camping gear, nothing but a leather bag that matched his jacket and smaller bags that probably carried camera equipment.

Of course, he could have left his camping gear wherever he'd moved his camp, but Manny had a hard time picturing this guy—with his shiny loafers and designer jeans—sleeping on the ground.

The guy tried twisting from his grasp, but Manny tightly held on to him. "I was told this is where she's staying," Setters protested. "I know she's here."

Manny snorted. "I hope you didn't pay for that tip."

The guy's face flushed with embarrassment. Apparently he had paid for the information. Would the stalker have sold Teddie's whereabouts?

Manny doubted it. He would have wanted to keep her all to himself, isolated, so he could get to her more easily, like he had the night before. No. Someone else must have recognized her around town. Or maybe even the people from whom she'd bought the cabin had sold her out.

Maybe she was right. She couldn't trust anyone.

"I heard you talking to somebody inside the cabin," the guy said, dragging those shiny loafers as Manny steered him around the hood toward the driver's door. "It sounded like her voice. I think she's here."

He sounded like he was trying really hard to convince himself of that.

Manny chuckled. "How much you pay for that tip?" he asked. "Because I can give you—"

Another vehicle turned from the street onto the long gravel drive leading toward the cabin. Through the trees Manny recognized the SUV his friends had rented from someone at the airstrip.

They had returned pretty quickly. It must not have taken them long to talk to the townspeople. Of course, from what Manny had seen the day before, it wasn't much of a town. The SUV pulled up behind the hatchback.

The reporter turned toward it with excitement and tried to lift his camera. But Manny locked his arm around Setters's arms, keeping them locked down at his sides.

He wriggled in his grasp. "Let me go! This is assault. I will have you arrested."

"And I'll have you arrested for trespassing."

Lars and Cole jumped out of the front of the SUV and started toward them. "This guy giving you a problem?" Lars asked as he arched a pale blond brow. His big body was tense, his hand close to his holster. He was silently asking if this was the stalker.

Manny shook his head and disappointment flashed through him. They apparently hadn't come back so soon because they'd learned the stalker's identity—not if they thought this guy could be the stalker.

"No problem at all," Manny said, "just some reporter that got duped. Old Bernie here thinks this cabin belongs to some guy named Teddie Plummer."

"Teddie Plummer is a supermodel!" Setters exclaimed, his voice sharp with indignation. Manny figured he was more indignant about being called old than about Teddie being mistaken for a man.

Amused, Manny pushed the joke and asked, "What— he model underwear or something?"

Setters jerked from his grasp and whirled around to face him. "He's a woman!"

Manny grimaced. "That's an awful name for a woman. She really that famous?"

"I wouldn't be here if she wasn't incredibly famous," the guy said. "I am Bernard Setters." He turned toward Cole and Lars as if checking their faces for signs of recognition.

They both shrugged their wide shoulders. "Never heard of you, buddy," Cole remarked. But Manny knew his friend was lying. He had recognized the name. Because he lowered his head and turned away from the reporter, probably hoping the guy wouldn't recognize him.

"Rednecks," Bernard muttered as he reached for his door handle. He glanced back at the SUV. "Can you back that thing up so I can get out of here?"

Cole nodded as he headed back toward the open driver's door. "Sure enough…"

Bernard glanced up at Manny. "I am sorry for bothering you," he said. "I'll let you get back to…" His eyes widened as he finally noticed their holsters. He tried to pull open the driver's door.

But Manny was there, his body blocking it from opening far enough for the guy to squeeze into the car. He wrapped his hands around the top of the door and lowered his voice to a deep growl. "Better verify your source a little more thoroughly next time."

The reporter's head bobbed in a quick nod. "Yeah, yeah..."

Manny stepped back and let the guy squeeze into his rental hatchback. But before the door closed, he heard Setters mumble something about Michigan militia. Once Cole pulled the SUV up beside instead of behind the hatchback, the reporter put the vehicle into Reverse and scrambled down the drive, spewing gravel behind the small tires.

Lars chuckled. "He won't be back."

"I'm not so sure," Manny said as the others stepped out of the SUV. Maybe they were the ones who'd been duped. "Her stalker being a reporter makes sense," he said. "That's how he always finds her—tips from sources. And that's how he has all those pictures."

"But if it was that reporter, why did he show up here like this?" Lars asked.

"Maybe he saw all you drive off and wanted to see if she was alone?" Dane was dark-haired and nearly as big as him; he could have been mistaken for Manny.

Nikki nodded. "It does make sense," she agreed.

"What did you guys turn up in town?" Manny asked, although he wasn't hopeful they'd learned much.

"That *Yoopers* don't like to talk to anyone from *downstate*," Cole said. "Whoever tipped off that reporter wasn't from around here."

"So you came up empty?" he asked. He'd figured as much with their quick return. But he was disappointed. He needed to wrap up this assignment soon—for Teddie's sake but also for his own.

"We need to bring her to River City," Cole said. "Get her the hell out of here where we can protect her better."

Frustration had Manny wanting to punch something. Maybe he shouldn't have let that reporter go so easily, especially if Bernard Setters was actually her stalker. "We need to catch this guy."

Nikki tilted her head and mused aloud, "Maybe we can do both…"

"You have a plan," her fiancé said as he narrowed his pale blue eyes and studied Nikki. "Why do I think I'm not going to like it?"

Nikki shrugged. "I'm actually hoping you don't like it too much."

A chill of unease chased down Manny's spine. Maybe the stalker was watching him from somewhere out in the woods. Or maybe Manny just had a premonition that he wasn't going to like Nikki's plan, either. And when it came to Nikki, it wouldn't matter that he was the lead on this assignment; she was the Payne.

They would all wind up going along with her plan no matter how dangerous it might prove to be.

Chapter 9

Lars Ecklund loved Nikki Payne more than he'd ever thought it possible he could love anyone. Not only was she brilliant, she was also beautiful—with short, curly auburn hair and big brown eyes. But he found himself ridiculously attracted to the woman sitting next to him in the back of the SUV that Cole was driving toward the airport.

Her hair was long and red and hung in loose curls around her shoulders. She wore dark glasses, as if she didn't want to be recognized. But how could she not be? That hairstyle had been named for her and wigs had been made to imitate it.

"You can stop staring now," she told him.

"I—I'm sorry…" he murmured. He knew he was getting in trouble, but he didn't care. His pulse hammered as desire overwhelmed him.

He leaned close and slid his hand over her thigh. Beneath the denim it was toned and warm.

Her lips curved into a slight smile. "I don't know whether I should be flattered or mad as hell."

He pulled his hand away. "I sure don't want you mad as hell."

Nikki Payne was dangerous when she wasn't angry. When she was…

Lars shuddered. "No, sweetheart, I certainly don't want you mad at me."

Nikki tipped the dark glasses down and peered at him over the top of them. "You really like the wig that much?"

He'd had a brief fantasy about her wearing it—and only it—when she'd packed it for their UP trip. She'd explained then that she might need to switch places with their client in order to protect Teddie Plummer. That had quickly cooled his interest in the wig.

He still wasn't thrilled when Nikki put herself in danger to protect others. But he knew it was as much a part of who she was as her quick wit and intelligence. And because he loved everything about her, he loved that, too. He was just happy that he was sitting close to protect her. He put his hand on her thigh again.

"You know I love you in everything." He leaned his head close to hers. "And in nothing at all."

"Ew," Cole said from the front seat. "Break it up. Nobody needs to see that." He lowered his voice and added, "Especially not me."

Nikki slid a little away from Lars. "Especially not the stalker."

Lars slid toward her so their thighs touched again.

"Or it might be good if he does, might piss him off enough to try for you."

"You really think the wig will fool him?" Nikki asked. She glanced down at the clothes she wore. "I don't look like a little girl playing dress-up?"

While she was petite and Teddie Plummer was not, Nikki had impressive curves of her own, which she'd displayed in a tight sweater.

"You definitely don't look like a little girl," Lars assured his sexy fiancée. But to his disappointment, Lars only caught glimpses of her figure beneath the long coat she wore. To add some height, she also wore boots with really high heels, so high that she'd had to clutch his arm to steady herself as they'd walked from the cabin to the SUV.

She'd also carried Teddie's purse while Cole had carried Teddie's luggage. Of course, it had all been empty.

"But do I look like Teddie?" she asked.

"The stalker couldn't be close to the cabin or we would have spotted him," Lars said. "So yeah, from a distance, you could pass for her."

Nikki nodded. "I'm hoping that's true."

She really wanted that sick son of a bitch after her rather than their client. Yeah, that was the woman he loved.

The sound of the SUV engine had died out long ago, leaving an eerie silence in the cabin. "They really all left?" Teddie nervously asked.

She wasn't worried about her safety. She was worried about being all alone with Jordan Mannes. She had already made a fool of herself when she'd kissed him. She was the one she didn't trust now. She wasn't certain what she might do next to him.

"Not all of them," Jordan said as he peered through the blinds.

She stepped up behind him, and his big body tensed. He knew she was there. Did the man have eyes in the back of his head? She peered at his thick, dark hair but could see nothing but temptation. She wanted to touch the strands to see if they were as soft as they looked. She curled her fingers into her palms and leaned closer to the window.

What she'd seen when she'd peered out earlier had scared her nearly as much as the stalker had. She'd seen Manny talking to Bernard Setters. And for a moment she'd felt betrayed, like she had when the other people she'd thought were her friends had spoken to the infamous tabloid reporter. Actually, she'd felt more betrayed, which was crazy. Jordan Mannes was not her friend. He was her bodyguard.

And he had proved that when he'd escorted the reporter—a little roughly—to his rental car. How had Bernard found her? How did he ever find her, though?

Nikki Payne had checked her cell phone and computer and all her other possessions for tracking devices. But the tech expert had declared everything free of bugs. Nobody had put a GPS on Teddie. Yet somehow they always knew where she was. The stalker, the paparazzi…

She shivered.

"You're cold," Jordan said. "You should step away from the window."

But she suspected he wanted her away from him more than from the window. His whole body seemed impossibly tense, like hers. Tension wound so tightly inside her. She couldn't sit. She couldn't read.

She could only worry. About the stalker.

And about Jordan Mannes.

She leaned closer, trying to peer over his shoulder. "Who's out there?" she asked. "I saw all your friends get into that SUV."

"Dane."

He'd been wearing dark glasses, a hat to hide his supershort hair and Manny's jacket. While Lars Ecklund had stood on one side of his fiancée, Dane had stood on the other. They'd been flanking her to fool the stalker into thinking Nikki was Teddie. But she'd thought the giant bodyguards only made the woman look smaller and less like her.

"Dane left with them," she said, her voice a little sharp. She hated being lied to. Yes, she would be a fool to trust Jordan Mannes.

"That's the impression we wanted to give to whoever's watching the cabin," Jordan explained. "But Dane doubled back and is out there. You're safe."

She shook her head. She wouldn't be safe until her stalker was caught and stopped.

Jordan turned away from the window and stared down at her. "I promise," he said, his brown eyes dark and intense. "I won't let him hurt you."

She nodded in appreciation that he would at least try to make her feel better. But she was disappointed that he would make promises he had no way of knowing he could keep. When she turned to walk back to the couch, he caught her arm.

Even through the thick material of her sweatshirt, she could feel the heat and strength of his fingers. He turned her back to face him. As if he'd read her mind, he said, "I don't make promises I can't keep."

"We all do," she said and tossed out some examples. "'I'll call.' 'I'll keep in touch.'"

He shook his head now. "Not me…"

And she wondered if he was talking about the promises or keeping in touch. Of course, he'd already warned her that he intended to remain single because he didn't trust his judgment. It sounded to her like he didn't trust women. He had trusted Nikki Payne, though.

"Do you really think this plan will work?" Teddie asked him. "Do you really think the stalker will mistake Nikki for me?"

He was silent for a long time—so long that she'd figured he didn't intend to answer her, just stare at her. While Nikki had been getting dressed in her disguise as Teddie, the female bodyguard had warned Teddie about how talkative *Manny* was. But Teddie had yet to see the garrulousness she'd been warned about.

Finally he opened his mouth and replied, "I sure as hell hope so."

He obviously wanted her stalker to be caught, too. But she wondered if his only reason was that he wanted her safe. Or was it that he wanted off this assignment?

Did he not want to protect her anymore?

Manny was mentally kicking himself. Before he'd left, Cole had made another offer to take over for him as the primary bodyguard. He should have accepted the offer, especially now.

Teddie was doing yoga. "You really don't mind?" she asked as she rolled out a mat in the space she'd cleared in front of the couch.

"No," he said.

She leaned over and began stretching. "I know I can't go outside, but I *really* need to burn off some energy."

Manny had some other ideas of how she could do that. As she wrapped one leg around the other, he imagined her wrapping both of those long legs around him. He suppressed a groan—barely—as his body reacted to the images in his mind.

Then she leaned over and peered at him between her thighs. "Did I hear you talking to someone?"

"Cole," he said. His friend had called from the airport while Teddie had been in the bathroom changing out of the baggy sweat suit and into the yoga pants and tank top that clung to her every sweet curve.

"Oh, did something happen?" she asked. "Did the stalker try to grab Nikki?"

"No."

She blew out a shaky-sounding breath. "The plan didn't work."

"Or he's not an idiot," Manny said. And he obviously wasn't or he would have been caught before now.

"I knew he wouldn't fall for Nikki's disguise."

"We don't know that he hasn't," Manny said. "He might have just been too smart to try for her with the guys present." And even if Nikki had insisted they leave her alone, for her protection they would have stuck close enough for the stalker to detect their presence.

"So are they coming back now?" she asked as she continued to hold the pose that was making Manny's jeans uncomfortably tight. She was on tiptoe and fingertips, her body bent over with her backside facing him.

He wanted to take her that way. Hell, he wanted to

take her any way he could have her. But guys like him didn't get lucky enough to make love to supermodels. Teddie Plummer had always been his fantasy woman, but even though he'd met her, she would continue to be just a fantasy. He didn't count that kiss she'd given him.

That had been gratitude for his protection. He knew better than to mistake her gesture for attraction or anything else.

"Are they coming back?" she asked again.

He shook his head and tried to focus on anything other than her distracting backside. "Uh, no. Cole's flying himself, Lars and Nikki in her Teddie disguise back to River City. They're hoping the stalker will follow them."

Cole had befriended the pilots at the airstrip, so he would get a call if anyone tried hiring them for a quick trip to River City. It wasn't as immediate a plan as the stalker just trying to grab decoy Teddie, but it still could lead to at least a description of her stalker.

"So we're staying here?" she asked, sounding less than thrilled.

"Are you already bored with the solitude?" he teased her.

Despite her claims, he believed her stalker had driven her from the bright lights of the big cities and her career. He couldn't believe she had willingly given it all up. Maybe he didn't want to believe this, but would rather keep her as a fantasy and nothing more.

"You're ready to return to civilization?" he asked.

Not that he would call River City civilization. Until recently, the city, which was as urban and populated as Detroit, had been full of crime and corruption. There had been nothing civilized about it. That was why the

Payne Protection Agency had gotten so well-known, for all the lives they'd saved and crimes they'd stopped.

She shuddered. "No. I wanted to stay here for a long time. I love this cabin, this area. But my solitude was shattered last night."

He wasn't certain what had shattered her solitude. The stalker or him?

"We won't be staying that much longer," he assured her and himself.

Being alone with her was pushing his control to limits Manny hadn't even known he had. Eventually it would exceed his limits.

"How will we get to River City?" she asked.

"I'll fly us," he said.

Cole had left his plane and returned to River City in the one he'd borrowed from the old crop-duster pilot, Walt. He'd said he'd done it because he'd promised Walt that no one would fly his plane but Cole. He might have done it because he wasn't sure Manny could handle the old temperamental machine as well as he could. Whatever his reason, Manny was relieved that he would be flying Teddie to River City in the newer, nicer and bigger plane.

"When you said you hadn't flown commercial, I thought you hired a private plane," she said. "I didn't realize you had actually piloted one yourself."

He shrugged. It was just something else he'd learned in the Marines, like how to shoot and fight and protect others. He'd needed those skills for the missions he and his unit had carried out. He hadn't realized how much he would need them as a bodyguard. He was especially glad he had them now, so he could protect Teddie.

But as she resumed her yoga moves, he hoped he

could protect himself from the desire he felt for her. Even though he had Dane for backup, he couldn't afford to be distracted now.

If the stalker hadn't fallen for Nikki's plan, then he was still out there, too—waiting to try again for Teddie.

Chapter 10

Manny was a pain in the ass. Dane glanced down at the text message his friend had sent on the new phones Nikki had brought up from River City. This wireless carrier got great reception in the UP, unfortunately.

Dane slid his gun into his holster so he could text Manny back.

Everything's fine. No sign of the stalker. Stop bothering me and get some sleep.

Hopefully it was just sleep deprivation making his friend so crazy. But Dane suspected it was the woman. When his girlfriend, Emilia, had been in danger, it had made Dane crazy. He'd been so worried about her. He would have done anything to keep her safe, even giving up his own life for hers.

But it wouldn't come to that for Manny. In the woods Dane had been patrolling, he had seen no sign of the stalker. Perhaps the guy had followed the SUV to the airport and Cole would get a call soon about who the stalker had hired to fly him to River City after them.

Dane couldn't wait to get this assignment wrapped up so he could go home to Emilia and their son, Blue. He slid the cell phone back into his pocket, next to the little velvet jewelry box he'd been carrying for the past couple of weeks.

He wanted everything to be perfect when he proposed. He wanted Emilia to have no doubts about his love and commitment to her and their son. Blue technically was just hers. But Dane had fallen as hard for the little boy as he had the baby's mother.

He hadn't intended to fall for her. He hadn't thought he was capable of loving anyone. But Emilia had given him no choice about giving his heart. She'd just taken it.

Manny swore he wasn't going to fall for anyone, either. But he didn't realize a guy didn't always have a choice. Sometimes the woman just took what she wanted. And from the way Teddie Plummer had kept looking at him, Dane wondered if the supermodel wanted his friend.

He snorted at his own ridiculous thought. She was a supermodel. And Manny...

Manny was just Manny. A pain in the ass.

A twig snapped behind him and brush rustled. He had a pretty good idea who'd ventured away from the house. Manny must not have been willing to take his word for it that nobody was in the woods but Dane and some animals. The guy had let this whole lead-bodyguard assignment thing go right to his head.

"Damn it, man," Dane said, "who died and made you the boss of Payne Protection?"

Manny didn't reply. And knowing his friend could never hold his silence made Dane realize it wasn't Manny he'd heard. He reached for his holster, but before he could draw his weapon, something hit him.

Hard.

In the head. Just before everything went black, he wished he'd proposed to the woman he loved—because now he might never get the chance.

The yoga had done nothing to ease the tension in Teddie's body. In fact, feeling Jordan's gaze on her as she had gone through each of the poses had only increased her tension. She was edgier now than she'd been before she'd started.

Anxious to escape the close confines of the cabin, she asked, "When can we leave?"

His brow furrowed slightly. "I'm not sure we should."

"What? We can't stay here," she said. "It's not safe."

He held up his phone, but it was too far away for her to read the text on it. "It might be safer here than anywhere else."

"Why? Did he follow them to River City?" If he had, she definitely didn't want to go there. But there had to be someplace else he could fly her.

Not that she was anxious to fly. Of course the stalker wouldn't be able to sneak on the private plane with them, but she would be confined with Jordan Mannes in a space even smaller than the cabin. And already he filled her senses—with his smell. It was nothing like the fragrance of the men she'd known who wore expensive colognes. It was soap and a scent that was his alone. Pheromones.

That was all it was.

And his heat. She could feel the warmth of his body even across the feet that separated them. It heated her own skin and made her pulse race.

"I don't know yet if he followed them," Jordan said, "but according to Dane's text, he's seen no sign of anyone in the woods. So your stalker's not hanging around here anymore. He must believe that you've left."

"Good." The pressure she'd had on her chest since the moment she'd received that first deranged note eased slightly. "That's good."

"Since we're safe here," Manny continued, "we should probably stay here."

And the pressure returned. "Are—are you going to switch with Dane?" she asked. Maybe if he went outside, she would be able to breathe again.

He shook his head. "Just in case Dane's wrong and the guy is still watching the place, we don't want him to see me. It's important that he think I left with you."

"But I thought Dane was dressed like you. Won't the stalker think he's you, anyway?"

"Dane's not wearing my coat anymore," Manny said, "and he took off the hat."

That disguise had been even weaker than Nikki's. Teddie never would have been able to mistake one man for the other. Dane was big and muscular. But he wasn't as big and muscular as Jordan was.

Teddie shook her head, and her hair tangled around her face. "I don't think anyone would be stupid enough to fall for either disguise." She reached up to push back her hair, but another hand was already there, a bigger hand.

For such a big man, Manny moved ridiculously fast. He pushed her hair off her face and tucked it behind her ears. She shivered as his fingertips brushed across her skin. What was it about this man that had her so intrigued, so attracted?

"What's wrong?" he asked, his deep voice even deeper with concern. "Are you upset about the disguises or about me?"

"I'm just frustrated," she admitted. "I want to get back to my life."

"The bright lights? The big cities?"

Her temper sparked now. He really seemed determined to think the worst of her. He claimed he didn't read tabloids, but she wondered. "I want to get back to the books, back to studying for my degree."

"Go ahead," he said, and he stepped back so he was no longer standing between her and the desk. "Study."

She shook her head. He was still standing between her and the books—at least in her mind. "I can't."

"Why not?"

"Because you're too distracting," she admitted.

His dark eyes widened, and he sucked in a breath. "What?"

"I'm frustrated because you're too damn distracting," she said and winced at the admission. She hated it when men said things like that to her. She couldn't believe she'd uttered something nearly as sexist.

But instead of being offended, Jordan Mannes laughed and shook his head. "Cole and Dane are right. I must be overly tired."

He had stayed up the entire night before, guarding

her. Maybe that was what she found so attractive about him—his protectiveness—even though he was getting paid to protect her. No. What she found so attractive about him was that he was so damn attractive.

He continued, "I thought I heard you call me..." But he shook his head. "Yeah, I'm too tired. Since Dane's guarding the outside, I probably should try to get some sleep."

She nodded. "You can use the loft," she offered. Maybe if he was out of her sight, he would be out of her mind. She doubted that, though, especially when he continued to study her face.

"You didn't say..."

She sighed. "Yes, I really said it. I find you distracting. Handsome. Sexy—"

His mouth covered hers, cutting off whatever embarrassing admission she'd been about to make, and he made love to her mouth. He nibbled at her lips, gently tugging and then stroking his tongue over the sensitive flesh. Then he deepened the kiss.

Teddie clutched at his shoulders and then the nape of his neck, holding his head down as she kissed him back. A kiss had never excited her so much, had never had every sensitive point of her body pulsing with need before as it pulsed right now. Tension wound inside her, tightening her nipples so they pressed against the thin material of her tank top.

As if he'd felt them, Jordan groaned. Despite her hands on his neck, he pulled back.

She tensed even more—with fear that he was about to reject her again. But instead of pushing her away, he swung her up in his arms.

"I think we should head to the loft," he said as he carried her up the steep and narrow steps.

She wasn't petite like Nikki Payne, but her weight didn't faze him in the least. His heavily muscled arms barely bulged as he carried her toward the bed. But his chest, his massive, muscular chest, moved as if he was breathing hard, or as if his heart was beating hard. Hers was, too, pounding against her skin.

She had never wanted anyone with this crazy desperation with which she wanted Jordan Mannes. He laid her on the bed but didn't follow her down. She tried to hold on to him, her arms clutching his shoulders. But he easily pulled away from her. She bit her lip so that she didn't cry out in protest. She needed him so badly. Her body throbbed in places she hadn't known she could feel.

But he didn't turn away from her. He stared down at her, his eyes both dark and hot with desire for her. Then he pulled off his holster and set it, with his weapon inside, onto the table next to the bed. Then, muscles rippling, he lifted his T-shirt and pulled it over his head and off. He unclasped his belt next, unbuttoned his jeans and wriggled them off along with his boxers. His erection sprang gloriously free.

She moaned as desire gripped her, tensing her stomach muscles into knots. "Manny…"

That was what his friends called him. And now she understood why. She had never seen more man than he was. Could she take him? All of him?

She sank her teeth into her lower lip as she contemplated it. But she had no time to decide because he was undressing her next. He lifted her tank top, with its built-in cups, over her head, freeing her breasts.

Then he hooked his fingers into her yoga pants and pulled them down her legs until she lay completely naked on the bed.

He gasped as he stared down at her. "I must be dreaming..." he murmured. "You can't be real."

People—designers, critics, men—often said that about her body. "They're not implants," she assured him.

He shook his head. "That's not what I meant." He reached out and touched her, sliding his fingertips along her side, over the curve of her hip and down her thigh.

Her breath caught, trapped in her lungs.

"You are so beautiful," he murmured almost reverently. "So *damn* beautiful..."

She knew that she was. She had been told so many times. But when he said it, it meant something to her. His compliment pleased her because it seemed genuine. He seemed genuine.

She reached out to touch him, skimming her hands over his washboard abs and down to his pulsing erection. She wrapped her fingers around him.

He gasped again.

"You're beautiful," she told him.

His lips curved into a slight grin as he breathed hard. Then he pulled back, out of her grasp.

And she nearly whimpered in frustration.

Suddenly he was there on the bed with her. But he didn't move quickly. He didn't fill that ache inside her, not with his erection. His fingers brushed across the most sensitive part of her body.

And she gasped now.

Then he was kissing her, his mouth over hers. His

lips skimmed back and forth before he began to tease her with his tongue. And his hands moved over her body, caressing her skin. He cupped her breasts in his big hands. His palms brushed across her nipples.

Sensations raced through her, and she bit her lip—or was it his? She gasped as her body shuddered with a slight release.

"Wow," he murmured. "You are so sensitive."

To his touch. Something about his hands on her body drove her wild. She shifted against the mattress, moving beneath him as she wanted more—more pleasure.

His hand moved, his thumb rotating over the part of her body that throbbed for him. Then his fingers moved inside her, stroking. She bit her lip—no, his—as she came again.

"You're driving me crazy," he said.

But she was the one out of her mind with pleasure. And still it wasn't enough.

Maybe she had denied herself too long. It had been a while since she'd had any kind of relationship with anyone. She hadn't trusted anyone enough to allow them this close, close enough to touch her.

She could trust Manny. His job was to protect her. He wouldn't hurt her. Yet a pang of fear struck her heart. She had never felt more vulnerable than she did now. The passion pushed the fear aside, and she clutched at his shoulders, pulling him closer.

"Manny, please," she implored him.

But he pulled back.

"Please!" she said as urgency gripped her. She needed him—needed to release the tension inside her.

She had been on edge for months, since that first

letter had arrived. But this was different. This was unbearable.

"Shh…" he murmured as he kissed her lips.

Was he pulling away? How did he have so much control? Was it because she hadn't touched him like he'd touched her? She reached for him now, but he stepped farther away. Then he leaned down and reached into his jeans pocket, pulling out a foil packet.

Her fingers trembling, Teddie reached for the packet. But he held tightly to it.

"If you roll this on me, it'll be all over," he warned her through gritted teeth.

And she realized he was fighting hard for that control she had thought so effortless. He rolled on the condom as far as it would go down his impressive length. Then he parted her legs and eased inside her.

He was so big.

But she was so ready for him. She arched and took him as deep as she could. And she had never felt as complete as she felt. She wrapped her legs around his waist and clutched his shoulders as they found a rhythm together. It was fast and frantic and furious.

She cried out as she came. But he kept moving.

And she came again.

Then finally his control slipped, and his body shuddered as he joined her in release. She melted into the mattress, boneless with pleasure.

He rose from the bed and slipped away, but only for minutes before he was back with her. His arms wound around her as he pulled her limp body against his.

She had never felt so safe, so protected, as she did in the arms of her bodyguard. She could only hope that her judgment had not been off this time, that she hadn't once again trusted the wrong person.

Manny was dreaming. He had to be dreaming. He couldn't have just made love to his fantasy woman. That was just a fantasy. That wasn't reality.

Not his reality.

A Mannes didn't have this kind of fortune. They only had misfortune. But she was lying in his arms, her body soft against his.

And warm.

And real.

He hadn't taken Dane's advice and fallen asleep and dreamed it all. It had actually happened.

And she'd wanted it. She had wanted him.

But why?

They had nothing in common. He was nothing like the rock stars and actors she'd been linked with in the tabloids. But then, she'd warned him not to believe everything he'd read about her.

He hadn't read anything about her growing up poor— like he had. With a single mother, like he had.

Maybe they had more in common than he'd realized. But that wasn't her life anymore.

She'd made another life for herself, one full of fame and fortune. He didn't want either of those things. He only wanted to do his job.

And his job was to keep her safe, not seduce her. He'd failed her. And himself.

He'd never felt happier about any failure before. He'd never felt anything like he had with her.

No. He had to be dreaming.

He lowered his head to her hair and breathed deep.

He expected the scent that had filled his nostrils all day, the scent that had been driving him out of his mind with desire for her.

He must have lost his mind to have carried her up to that loft and joined her on the bed. He was her bodyguard. Not her boyfriend.

For the moment, though, with her lying in his arms, he could pretend that he was more to her than just her protector. But when he breathed in, he didn't smell her, that scent of flowers and sunshine.

Instead he coughed and sputtered as smoke filled his nose. It wafted up to the loft from below.

The damn cabin was on fire.

Manny knew that it was no accident. They had left no logs smoldering in the small woodstove. Nor had any candle been burning when he'd carried her up the stairs and gotten carried away himself. The only fire that had been burning then had been between the two of them.

So the cabin hadn't started on fire accidentally. Someone had set it on fire. When Manny had lost his mind and made love to his client, he'd let down his guard. And he'd put her life and his own in danger.

Would he be able to get her out alive?

And even if he did, he had no doubt that the stalker was out there—waiting for them. So he could strike when they were most vulnerable. And with Teddie in his arms, Manny had never been more vulnerable.

Chapter 11

How the hell could she do this to him? First she'd tried to trick him—sending some other woman off dressed like her, wearing a wig. Had Teddie really thought he would fall for that cheap imitation of her?

Didn't she realize how well he knew her?

Maybe he didn't know her as well as he'd thought he had. Because she'd never dated the male models or actors or rock stars who had asked her out, he'd thought she wasn't into superficial relationships. He'd assumed she was looking for something meaningful, with someone worthy of her. So how could she betray him with some muscle-bound thug like that bodyguard?

He'd heard her cry out. He knew what they had been doing inside the cabin. That was why he'd struck the match. He'd rather burn her down than lose her to someone else.

But he didn't expect them just to perish quietly inside the cabin. That damn bodyguard would try to play the hero. He would be rushing out of the fire soon with her in his arms.

And he would be ready for him.

He lifted the weapon he'd taken from the other bodyguard, the one he'd left to die in the woods. The gun was heavy and unfamiliar in his hands. But he knew to slide off the safety before pulling the trigger.

And as soon as that bodyguard stepped out of the cabin, he would pull the trigger. He would shoot a bullet right into that pseudo hero's pea-sized brain.

If Teddie was lucky, he might let her live for a while, at least long enough to make it up to him for betraying him like she had. But first the bodyguard had to die.

"Wake up," a deep voice ordered. "You need to wake up."

Teddie tried to open her eyes, but her lids were so heavy. Then her eyes began to burn and water like they had with the pepper spray. Her nose burned, too, but it was smoke filling her nostrils and her lungs. She coughed and sputtered.

But even as she realized there was smoke, she could summon no energy and none of the urgency she heard in Manny's voice. She was too satiated. Too limp.

After making love with him, she'd slipped into a sleep so deep that she couldn't shake it off. Or maybe it was smoke that was making her listless.

Manny moved her, lifting her arms, sliding them into sleeves as he pulled a sweatshirt over her head. Then he dragged pants up her thighs. He dressed her even faster than he'd undressed her earlier.

"Teddie, we need to get out of here," he told her. "The cabin's on fire."

Finally his words penetrated the fog in her brain. She wasn't certain if the smoke had caused it or the incredible sex. But she shook it off now.

"What!" She jumped up but the smoke was thick in the loft, blinding and overwhelming her. She coughed and sputtered again. "Fire…"

Not the cabin. Not her little sanctuary.

But it hadn't felt like a sanctuary since the stalker had chased her from the woods. He had destroyed it even before he'd set it on fire. It must have been him.

He hadn't left like they'd hoped he would. He hadn't been fooled. In fact, he was probably angry that they had tried to fool him.

Strong arms lifted her, and as easily as he'd carried her up the steps earlier, Manny carried her down. The smoke was thinner downstairs. So she could see the glow of flames behind the blinds, licking up the outside of the structure.

Then glass cracked and shattered and the flames forced their way inside, melting the blinds. Thick, black smoke billowed from them.

And now she was all urgency as fear overwhelmed her. "We need to get out of here!"

She was surprised she had to say it, surprised that Manny hesitated with her in his arms. They couldn't stay inside the cabin, not with the fire.

"He's out there," he said.

"Dane?"

He cursed. But he wasn't just angry. He sounded scared, too.

"I don't know where Dane is…" His fear was for his

friend. "But your stalker is out there. He set this fire to get us out there—with him."

His fear was for her, too.

"What...?" She coughed. "What are we going to do?" They couldn't stay inside much longer. If the smoke didn't kill them first, the flames definitely would.

Moments before, she'd felt so safe, asleep in his arms. Now she was terrified that they were both about to die. She had trusted Manny to protect her. Now she was afraid that she had made a horrible mistake.

Manny knew he was asking too much of her. He was asking her to trust him.

She stared up at him through eyes streaming from smoke. Blinking furiously, she asked, "You want me to stay inside—with the fire?"

She sounded shocked and horrified.

He felt the same way.

He could not believe he had let down his guard. He'd kept checking with Dane because he'd known—he'd just *known*—that the stalker hadn't been fooled. There was no mistaking Nikki for Teddie Plummer no matter how good the female bodyguard's disguise had been.

So what the hell had he been thinking to make love to the client? No matter how much Dane had assured him that he'd seen nothing amiss in the woods, Manny should have kept his own watch, as well. He shouldn't have let himself get distracted from his assignment.

"You just need to stay inside until I draw his fire," he explained.

"What?" She choked on the question, her lungs no doubt filling with smoke.

Manny carried her to the bathroom near the back

door of the cabin. It wasn't on fire. Yet. But the smoke was thick here, too. He soaked towels with which they covered their mouths, but it wasn't enough to filter out all the smoke.

He coughed, too.

He didn't have time to explain his plan again, not if they were going to survive. "Wait here, just until you hear fifteen shots."

She gasped. "Fifteen?"

That would empty the chamber of the Glock 19 that Dane carried. Because if the stalker was out there, he had gotten past Dane. And the only way he could have done that was if he'd killed him. Pain clasped Manny's heart in a viselike grip.

He'd been there when Dane had chosen the ring for Emilia, the ring his friend hadn't given her yet. Now he would never get the chance. And if Dane was dead, Manny had to assume the stalker had his gun.

He could not afford to be surprised again. It could cost them both their lives as it had probably cost Dane his.

"Stay here," he told her, opening the bathroom door. The fire had started on the deck. There was no going out the patio doors. "Fifteen shots."

The stalker wouldn't buy Manny going outside alone, so he carried a cushion from the couch wrapped in one of the blankets. Another blanket—soaked with water— was wrapped around Teddie. He kissed her, then pulled it over her face before he left her, closing the bathroom door on her. Hopefully she would remember his direction to roll the other wet towel he'd left in there against the bottom of the door to keep out more smoke.

Slinging the big pillow over his shoulder, he drew

in a deep breath then opened the back door. The minute he stepped out onto the small porch, shots rang out. Thankfully they were fired in quick succession and not very accurately. He didn't know if the stalker was a good shot or a bad one, though. He probably didn't want to hit Teddie. And with the blanket wrapped around the cushion, he might believe that Manny carried her.

He continued to fire, though. The bullets struck the gravel around the porch and then the cabin wall. Manny ran from the house, wanting to draw the gunfire away from it so Teddie wasn't accidentally struck. And so he wouldn't be hit, either. Ducking low, he headed away from the bathroom wall, toward the storage barn where Teddie had parked her Jeep and he had stowed the motorcycle.

Glancing over his shoulder, he could see the flash in the darkness and knew from where the shots were being fired. The shooter stood in the area where Manny had found Teddie that first night, where he had attacked Teddie that first night, somewhere between the house and the thicker woods.

Manny waited until he heard the fifteenth shot ring out and then the telltale click of an empty cartridge before he dropped the cushion onto the ground and drew his own weapon. He fired toward the trees as he started toward them.

Before going too far, he glanced back to make certain Teddie had followed his directions. The back door stood ajar as he'd left it, but she didn't come out. Maybe opening the door had fueled the fire with more oxygen.

She could have been overcome with the smoke or with the flames themselves. His heart pounded furiously with fear and dread. In trying to save her, had he been the one to kill her?

He headed back toward the cabin, hoping he hadn't left Teddie to burn alive inside it. But he found her exactly where he'd left her, just inside the bathroom door.

"What's wrong?" he asked. "Why didn't you come outside?" But he had to shout for his voice to be heard. The flames had risen in the rest of the house, roaring as they consumed the old wood.

"I didn't hear the shots," she said from where she crouched on the shower floor, still covered with that wet blanket.

He lifted and carried her out of the bathroom and out the back door. But as he stepped through it, something hard struck him. The heavy metal object missed his head and just glanced off his shoulder.

The son of a bitch had returned.

Manny jumped off the little porch and onto the gravel walk. Setting Teddie on her feet, he whirled toward the stalker. Even with the light from the fire dissipating the darkness, the man was only a shadow. A shadow with a gun. He must have grabbed only that, though, and not Dane's extra rounds of ammo. Because he swung the gun, handle out toward Manny, instead of pulling the trigger.

Manny dodged the blow. Then he drew his own weapon. The man turned and ran toward the trees. Manny had the shot. He could fire, yet he hesitated. It was hard for him to shoot a man in the back. So he aimed for a leg instead.

As he squeezed the trigger, a whimper distracted him. He didn't look to see if he'd hit his target before he turned back to Teddie.

She had collapsed on the gravel, the light from the flames illuminating her pale face. Her eyes were closed as if she'd slipped into unconsciousness. Or had staying inside the cabin, with all that smoke, damaged her lungs?

"Teddie!" He dropped to the ground beside her. His fingers shaking, he reached out for her throat, checking for a pulse. He found one, but compared to how it had raced earlier, it felt weak.

He lowered his head to her mouth but felt just a brush of her breath against his skin. She was breathing, but not that strongly, not that steadily.

He needed to get her to a hospital. But he had only the motorcycle to ride. She had her Jeep, though—safe with the motorcycle in the storage shed. The keys for it were inside the house.

He peered around, checking to see if the stalker lurked, waiting for another chance to strike like a hyena going for the weakest victim.

Dane wasn't the weakest, though. Dane was the toughest man Manny had ever met, tougher even than him. How the hell had the stalker overpowered the ex-Marine?

And where the hell was Dane?

The stalker was gone. If Manny had struck him, it hadn't been a painful enough wound to stop him from running. Hopefully it would stop him from coming back—at least until Manny was able to get the keys from inside the cabin.

Just as he headed toward it, the structure gave an ominous groan as if it were human. Flames broke through the roof, which then collapsed in on itself.

Her little cabin, and everything inside it, was gone.

Manny reached for his pocket, patting it. He had the keys to the motorcycle. But how could she hold on to him when she could barely keep her eyes open?

He pulled out his cell phone. He had no new messages from Dane, just the last one in which he had assured Manny that everything was all right. But had Dane typed that or had the stalker?

In addition to Dane's gun, the stalker probably had his phone. So Manny wouldn't send a text. He wouldn't even try to call him. Instead he punched in 911, and he hoped the signal was strong enough to get the call through. He had no idea if there was a fire or police department anywhere in the area. Would help arrive in time?

She needed oxygen, at least. Or maybe even more medical treatment. And he had no idea about Dane. Was it already too late to help him?

Chapter 12

Lungs burning, Teddie coughed and sputtered for air. Finally she was able to suck in a deep breath of it, which made her cough and sputter some more as she regained consciousness. Her eyes burned, too, and watered; she blinked and tried to clear her vision.

She was moving. But her feet weren't touching the ground. Someone was carrying her. For a moment she tensed with fear. Had the stalker gotten her?

She remembered Manny carrying her out of the burning cabin. But he'd been hit. Something had struck him. She'd heard his grunt. The stalker had been out there, waiting for him just as he'd warned her.

But hadn't Manny fought him off?

She couldn't remember what had happened after he'd set her on her feet. Her legs had refused to hold her weight and had folded beneath her. She'd dropped to the ground. She'd been barely able to gasp for breath, and consciousness had slipped away from her, rendering her unable to help Manny or herself.

She began to struggle now, but the arms of the man holding her tightened around her and a deep, familiar voice murmured, "Shh…it's okay. I'm getting you farther away from the fire, so you can breathe."

"Manny," she murmured and began to cough again. The coughing expelled some smoke from her burning lungs, making room for clean air. She gasped, trying to get more.

"Shh…" he said. "Help's on the way. They have a fire department up here and a state police post."

But she heard no sirens. The fire made the only sounds in the usual silence of the nights up here. It popped and hissed as it consumed what was left of the cabin.

She would be fine. She didn't need the help. "Dane…?"

What had happened to the other bodyguard?

"I—I don't know where he is," Manny said, his deep voice gruff with concern and pain.

Fear and guilt overwhelmed Teddie. The other man was missing because of her, because he had been trying to protect her. She wriggled in Manny's arms, trying to get him to release her.

But he held her tightly as he continued to carry her toward the street, where the fire trucks and police vehicles would arrive if they could find the cabin, or what was left of it.

"Go," she said, choking on the word and the guilt overwhelming her. Clearing her raw throat, she implored him, "Please go. Find him."

Manny shook his head. "I can't leave you."

Blinking against the tears streaming from her irritated eyes, Teddie stared up at his face. It was smoke-smeared and taut with anger and fear. A muscle twitched along his tightly clenched jaw. He was clearly torn.

"I'm fine," she assured him. But even as she said it, she dissolved into a fit of coughing. Her lungs ached. Her throat burned. She wasn't fine. But she was alive. Thanks to Manny. What about his friend?

"You won't be fine if the stalker comes back again," he said. "I can't leave you here alone and unprotected."

And she couldn't ask him to leave her the gun again, like he had when he'd taken the shower the first night. She couldn't send him off alone and unarmed into the woods. The stalker had just tried twice to kill him— first shooting at him and then attacking him as he'd carried her out of the fire.

Even though he'd survived those assaults, Jordan Mannes wasn't invincible. Nobody was.

"You need to find Dane," she said. "He needs help." He must or he would have come out of the woods by now. Certainly he would have when he'd seen the fire. How hurt was he?

That muscle twitched along Manny's rigid jaw again. "Dane's tough," he said, as if trying to convince himself. "You can't believe the things he's survived…" His voice trailed off before he rallied and added, "He has to survive this, too."

But they had no way of knowing what *this* was. What had the stalker done so that Dane had not come to their aid?

A noise rose above the sounds of the fire. It wasn't the rustle of brush of someone coming toward them on foot. This was the wail of sirens as flashing lights appeared on the road. Blue and red reflected off the tree trunks. Just as Manny had promised, help had arrived.

For her.

"You can leave now," she told him.

But he continued carrying her until they stood on the shoulder of the rural road. When an ambulance stopped, he walked her toward the back of it. The paramedics jumped out and hurried over to them.

"She's inhaled a lot of smoke," he told them. And as he said it, he coughed, too.

"What about you?" one of the paramedics asked. He had a beard, like so many of the Yoopers she'd encountered since moving to the cabin. Yoopers were what the people living in the Upper Peninsula of Michigan called themselves.

A pang struck her heart. Her cabin was gone. But that was the least of her concerns right now. How was Manny? Had he been hurt in the fire or by the stalker? She'd only assumed he was fine because he was taking care of her. But with his strength and resolve, he could have been shot and still carried her effortlessly.

The paramedic studied him with concern, which raised Teddie's.

After placing her on the stretcher that the other paramedic pulled from the back of the ambulance, Manny shrugged. "I'm fine."

"What happened?" A state trooper asked the question as he joined them. "Chimney fire?"

"Arson," Manny said. "She has a stalker who's trying to kill her. I'm her hired bodyguard."

She flinched at the reminder. After making love

with him, she needed it, though. She needed to remember that he was only doing his job.

The trooper's eyes widened with shock. "What—who are you?"

"I'll explain later," Manny said. "But another bodyguard from my agency is missing. I need to find him." He hesitated, still standing by her side.

Teddie followed Manny's gaze to the trooper, whom he was studying as if trying to determine if he could trust the man to protect her. The guy was older, his beard gray like the hair peeking out from his hat. But he looked fit, and he was armed.

"Stay with her," he told the trooper, who must have passed Manny's inspection. "Don't let her out of your sight."

After giving the order, he was immediately gone from her own sight, disappearing into the woods that Dane had been patrolling. Was he still out there? Was the stalker?

She wasn't certain what had happened after she'd lost consciousness. She wasn't sure where the man had gone after he'd attacked Manny again. But she suspected he hadn't gone far. He could be in the woods, waiting for Manny to come looking for him.

A paramedic held out an oxygen mask toward her, but she pushed it away as she turned toward the trooper. "Go with him," she said. "Help him!"

The trooper shook his head and shuddered a little. "I don't think *he* needs help. And I'm damn well not going to piss him off."

She knew how big Manny was, but she hadn't realized he could be intimidating until she saw the fear on the faces of the men around her.

Unfortunately, her stalker was not intimidated. He kept trying again and again to hurt Manny. Of course, he was crazy and obsessed. So he would not quit until he succeeded.

The paramedics slipped the mask over her mouth and nose, then loaded her into the back of the ambulance. The state trooper climbed in beside her. As the doors closed, she peered off into the darkness. But she could see only the smoke and the faint glow of the dying fire.

She could see no sign of the man who had saved her life. Her bodyguard. Jordan Mannes was gone.

Would she ever see him again?

Manny had watched until the trooper climbed in with Teddie and the ambulance had pulled away before he'd headed deeper into the woods. The men had done as he'd directed.

Teddie was safe.

Dane was not.

Where the hell was he? Concern tightened his stomach into knots. The guy had survived so much during their missions as Marines and their assignments as bodyguards. Hell, a bunch of gang members had been hired to jump Dane and later abduct him, and they'd all wound up hurt far worse than he'd been.

Dane was indestructible. But his mantra had always been that he wouldn't be taken alive.

If the stalker had taken out Dane Sutton, the man was far more dangerous than Manny had realized. So he had to move silently through the woods when he wanted to call out instead, yelling Dane's name. That would only put him in danger. And Manny wouldn't be able to help Dane or protect Teddie if he was dead.

Was she safe?

The stalker had to have a vehicle stashed somewhere nearby his campsite. He could have driven off after the ambulance. Sure, the trooper had had a gun. But would he fire it? Had he ever been in a situation where he'd needed to?

This area was so remote that there probably hadn't been much crime. Until now.

Now there was assault. And arson.

And murder?

Was Dane dead?

Away from the glow of the fire, the woods were dark and thick with the smoke that filled it like the fog had the night before. With so much smoke already in his lungs, Manny couldn't fight back the cough that burned his throat. The sharp noise shattered the eerie silence of the woods.

Gripping his Glock tightly, he tensed, waiting for something or someone to move in the darkness. But he heard nothing, saw nothing.

Until it was too late.

A strong arm locked around his throat, cutting off his breath far more effectively than the smoke had. And the muscles and strength in that arm were likely to crush his windpipe and kill him.

He tried to raise his gun, tried to direct the barrel behind him. But consciousness was already beginning to slip away from him.

At least he knew the stalker hadn't followed Teddie to the hospital. Instead the stalker was going to send him there or maybe straight to the grave.

* * *

Frustration gripped Cooper. "What the hell were you all thinking?" he asked, but the question was directed at the one he suspected was behind the ill-conceived plan.

Nikki shifted slightly in her chair around the conference room table. It had definitely been her plan.

"We were thinking that we would catch this damn stalker," Lars said, jumping to his fiancée's defense.

But Nikki was too proud to let anyone take the blame for her. She put her hand over Lars's on the conference room table and patted it. "*I* thought we could lure the stalker away from the cabin and Teddie."

"We don't know that it hasn't worked," Lars said, unwilling to stop defending his bride-to-be.

Cole snorted, though. He'd obviously had his doubts about the plan. "He never tried for us."

"That doesn't mean he didn't follow us," Nikki persisted. She'd always had a problem admitting when she was wrong.

Cooper cursed. "The stalker must love this."

"What?" Cole asked.

"You split the team in half," he pointed out.

"Not quite half," Nikki began, as she considered herself every bit as much a bodyguard as the ex-Marines. That she had proved, though, over and over again. Then she must have realized why Cooper was so upset. "We left less than half the team with the client." She cursed now.

Lars chuckled. "You call Manny and Dane less than half? They're both strong as hell. No damn stalker is going to take out either one of them, let alone both of them."

"True." Cooper's frustration eased slightly, taking

away some of the pressure that had been pushing on his chest and shoulders. He'd been having one of those crazy feelings his mom was notorious for getting, almost like a premonition, that something was wrong. But with Dane and Manny on the assignment, the client had to be safe.

Then his phone dinged. And the pressure was back, so intense that he could barely breathe. He glanced down at the text on his phone. It wasn't from Manny or Dane, though. It was from his brother Logan.

Your team on the news again?

"What is it?" Nikki asked, and all the color had drained from her face, leaving it nearly as pale as her fiancé's pale blond hair.

"I don't know." But he doubted it was good. His hand shook as he picked up the TV remote from the tabletop and clicked on the big screen mounted on one of the conference room walls.

A breaking news report had interrupted whatever late-night talk show would have been playing. Cooper didn't know what would have been on; he was usually in bed with his beautiful wife at this hour.

"An arson fire in a remote area of Michigan's Upper Peninsula nearly claimed the life of supermodel Teddie Plummer tonight," the news anchor said as the image of a burning cabin filled the screen behind him. "While Ms. Plummer was taken to a local hospital for smoke inhalation, her bodyguard disappeared in the woods while searching for another bodyguard."

Cooper's heart slammed against his ribs while the others gasped.

"Apparently, before his disappearance, Ms. Plummer's bodyguard warned local authorities that she has a stalker who had allegedly started the fire."

Cole cursed.

"Tabloid reporter Bernard Setters was in the area on a tip that Teddie Plummer had bought the cabin. He took these photos at the scene." More images flashed behind the anchor of the burning cabin and of Teddie Plummer, her beautiful face smeared with smoke, being loaded into the back of an ambulance.

Now their client was totally unprotected. But more important, where the hell were Dane and Manny, and what the hell had happened to them?

Chapter 13

"Damn it, man, I'm sorry…" The apology Dane uttered to Manny reverberated inside his own shattered skull. Well, it wasn't shattered. Just fractured from where the rock had struck the back of it. At least, that was what the CT scan had shown the ER doctor, just a hairline fracture and a concussion. The blood on the rock had shown Dane what that son of a bitch had used to knock him out cold.

He didn't even know how long he'd been out when he'd awakened to the smell of smoke filling the woods.

Manny pulled the oxygen mask away from his face and said, "Stop it…" But his voice was only a faint rasp.

Dane shuddered at how close he'd come to killing his friend. He'd awakened so disoriented and nearly blind with pain that he hadn't recognized Manny right away. He'd seen a big shadow with a gun sneaking through the woods and had just wanted to disarm him. Fortunately, he'd recognized his friend before he'd done more harm. It was lucky for him that Manny had recognized him even sooner and lowered his gun before he'd pulled the trigger. Or the CT scan would have shown a bullet in his brain.

Manny was a damn good shot.

But Dane wasn't relieved so much as he was guilt-ridden. "I'm sorry," he said again. But he wasn't apologizing just for choking Manny in the woods. He knew his friend would understand that. He was sorry about failing his assignment, about failing to guard Manny and their client. "I don't know how the hell he got the jump on me."

Manny's eyes darkened with more anger than Dane had ever seen in him before. "He's one dangerous son of a bitch." Beneath the soot smeared across it, his face paled. "I need to check on Teddie."

But when he tried to slide off the gurney and get to his feet, his legs folded beneath him. He would have fallen if Dane hadn't jumped up and grabbed his arm.

"You need more oxygen," the doctor said. "Your level is very low. And you may have damage to your lungs from the smoke inhalation."

But Manny wasn't worried about himself. He was worried about Teddie Plummer. Just because she was their client or because she had begun to mean something more to him?

Teddie had been moved from the emergency room to a private room shortly after arriving at the hospital. She wasn't certain if the doctor had ordered it or if the Michigan state trooper had requested it. He stood just inside the door, watching over her as nurses came in and out of her room. She was still on oxygen, and she'd been administered some type of breathing treatment to get the smoke out of her lungs.

While she was feeling physically better, emotionally she was a wreck. As if he saw her anxiety, the trooper reminded her, "The bodyguards have been found."

And she was glad about that. But she had to know… "Are they all right?"

He shrugged. "They're being treated in the ER."

Treated. So they had injuries. She sucked in a breath. "They're hurt, then."

But of course Dane had been hurt, or the stalker wouldn't have gotten past him to set the cabin on fire. And Manny had been in the fire and had fought with the stalker. He could have had any number of injuries—even a gunshot wound—that he hadn't told her he'd had.

He was that tough.

That professional.

Except for when he'd made love with her. That had not been professional behavior for either of them. She had hired him to protect her, not sleep with her. But still, she'd kissed him first. She was the one who had crossed the line. Then he had carried her the rest of the way over it.

She tried to swing her legs from under the blanket, but when she moved she started coughing again. She needed Manny to carry her now. She felt the loss of his presence, which was crazy given how short a time she'd known him.

In that time, she'd come to count on him, and that was what was crazy. She'd learned long ago never to count on anyone—even her mother. Mama had tried so hard to take care of them both, but she had struggled to support them on her own. They'd always been on the verge of losing the house and going hungry. Through babysitting and then modeling, Teddie had had to learn to take care of herself and her mother.

Now she wanted to take care of Jordan Mannes, and it wasn't just because they'd made love. She knew that had been a mistake. Since the stalker had begun terrorizing her, she'd felt so cut off and alone. She'd just needed to feel close to someone again—safe. Hell, she'd just needed to feel anything other than fear again.

And she'd certainly felt a lot with Manny. More pleasure than she'd thought possible. She'd also felt something else she'd never felt before: complete. But that was crazy. The stalker had probably driven her crazy. She wasn't falling for her bodyguard.

The reason she wanted to make sure Manny was okay was that she owed him. He had saved her life more than once.

"I need to know how he's doing," she said, and then she felt a pang of guilt for not thinking about his friend and amended, "How they're both doing. Can you find out for me?"

"I'm sure he'll come to you as soon as he's done being treated," the trooper replied.

She was, too. But he hadn't come yet, and that was what frightened her, that he wasn't physically able.

"Please," she implored him. "I'm really worried about him and the other bodyguard—Dane Sutton. I need to know how they're doing."

The trooper shook his head. "He told me to stay with you." And the guy had stuck to his promise to do just that.

"But we're in a hospital," she said. "Nobody will try anything here."

"I do need to get his statement," the trooper murmured.

He had already taken hers. She'd told him everything she knew, everything she had endured. Maybe that was why he hesitated to leave her. She'd told him too much.

"Yes, you should talk to Jordan Mannes," she said. "I don't know what happened when he went outside. Shots were fired." Or so she assumed. She hadn't been able to hear anything over the roar of the fire consuming the cabin around her. "And he may have gotten a look at the guy."

"You really haven't ever seen his face?" the trooper asked. He sounded almost skeptical that she didn't know who the stalker was.

Did he think she was one of those celebrities who would do anything to get in the headlines, even burn down her own cabin? She knew fame whores who'd done things like that—staged robberies, assaults, stalkings... all just to get their names in the news again.

Maybe that was why the police had never found him. They hadn't believed her, so they hadn't bothered looking for him—like Manny and the Payne Protection Agency had looked for him. She needed this trooper to believe her, though, so that he would talk to Manny.

"The times the stalker has been close enough for me to see, he's been wearing a ski mask," she said. "I haven't been able to see his face. Maybe Manny or his friend was able to get a better look at him."

The trooper nodded with understanding. "Then we could get a description out there. I'll go take their statements." He opened the door to the hall but turned back. "You're sure you'll be fine alone?"

She smiled as another nurse walked in to check her blood pressure. "I'm not alone."

The medical staff was keeping a close eye on her. The stalker wouldn't risk trying something in a busy hospital. The trooper must have concluded the same thing because he finally left her alone.

"Now that he's gone, you should try to get some rest," the nurse told her as she left, too.

But Teddie wouldn't be able to rest until she knew that Manny was okay, that he hadn't been badly hurt. She leaned back against the pillows, though, and closed her eyes, just to rest them. Irritated from the smoke, her eyes hurt so badly. She hadn't shut them for more than a second when she heard the door open again, noise spilling in from the hallway.

So much for telling her to get some rest when they wouldn't leave her alone.

With a sigh, she opened her eyes to see what they needed to check this time. But even though this person was dressed in scrubs, she doubted he actually worked for the hospital. A scrub hat covered his head and a mask his face. But she recognized the eyes peering over the mask. She had seen those eyes before when she'd been attacked.

She was wrong. Her stalker would obviously risk anything to get to her.

"You really never got a look at him?" Manny asked, frustration eating at him. He needed to get to Teddie and make sure she was okay. But not only were his own oxygen levels low, he was also concerned about Dane. The guy had taken one hell of a blow to his head.

"I didn't even have a chance to see stars, he hit me so hard," Dane replied. "I don't know how the hell he got the jump on me."

The guy had been sneaking around for a while, stalking Teddie probably even before she'd realized it.

"He's gotten good at being invisible," Manny mused.

Dane uttered a ragged sigh. "It's going to be hard to catch this guy when we have no clue who the hell he is."

"We'll figure it out," Manny assured him. They had to. Teddie wouldn't be safe until the guy was caught.

Or dead…

"I think I hit him," he said as he replayed the recent events through his mind.

"So you must have gotten a good look at him," Dane said.

"I mean with a bullet," Manny explained. "He was running away."

"And you shot him in the back?" It wasn't Dane who asked the question. He would know better. The voice came from the man who pulled back the ER curtain.

"No," Manny said. "I was aiming for one of his legs. I wanted to stop him. Not kill him." But he could have killed him—if he'd wanted. He had been trained for the kill shot, and he'd never missed before.

But Teddie had distracted him as she'd crumpled to the ground unconscious. So he didn't know if he'd actually hit one of the stalker's legs or not. He certainly hadn't stopped him. Probably the only way to do that would be to kill the guy. Maybe he should have taken that shot…

"Why are you here?" Manny asked with sudden alarm

as he recognized the trooper with whom he'd trusted Teddie. Of course, he wasn't the only state trooper in Michigan. Maybe this trooper had turned her protection over to another trooper or hospital security—although as small as this hospital was, Manny doubted they had much of a security staff.

"I need to get your statement," the trooper said. He turned toward Dane. "And yours. What the hell happened out there? I spoke to Ms. Plummer and I still don't know."

Manny heard the skepticism in his voice. "This isn't a stunt," he assured the lawman. "Ms. Plummer isn't looking for publicity." She would rather avoid it.

Dane touched the bandage on the back of his head. "I can definitely vouch for that."

"So you saw the stalker?"

"No," Dane admitted. "He hit me from behind. I've got the rock. Maybe you can get prints off it." The rock, smeared with soot and Dane's blood, sat on the table beside Dane's gurney. It was probably one of the rocks that had encircled the campfire Manny had found that first night in the woods.

"I'll have a tech process it," the trooper said.

Manny had a feeling their guy wasn't in the system. If he was someone invisible, like Manny suspected, then the stalker had never been caught before. He intended to change that, though, and soon.

"And what about you?" the trooper asked Manny. "Did you ever get a look at his face?"

Manny shook his head. "I can't tell you much about the guy. He's about six feet tall, lean build…"

The trooper glanced at the two of them, as if he wondered how some skinny guy had overpowered either of them. Manny wondered, too, but then, the guy was crazy, and crazy gave some people an almost superhuman strength and courage no matter what their size.

"We need to check with the hospital," Manny said, "and see if anyone's come in with a gunshot wound."

The trooper nodded. "So you think you might have hit him…"

"Manny doesn't miss," Dane answered for him.

But Manny shook his head. This time was different. Teddie had distracted him. From the moment he'd seen her, Teddie had distracted him. Hell, even before he'd met her, she had been a distraction for him.

A fantasy.

Once he'd discovered she was the client, he had had no business staying on this assignment. If he'd taken Cole up on relieving him, the stalker might have already been caught. And Teddie wouldn't be suffering from smoke inhalation. She wouldn't have been touched at all.

Especially not like he'd touched her. And kissed her. And held her.

"I'll check with admissions," the trooper assured him.

An uneasy feeling gripped Manny, and he had to ask, "You didn't leave her alone, did you?"

The trooper's face flushed. "She pleaded with me to check on the two of you."

Manny surged up from the gurney. And this time he was so mad and scared that his legs held his weight. He reached for the holstered weapon, which he'd left on the little cart next to his gurney.

"It's a hospital," the trooper said. "Doctors and

nurses are going in and out of her room. He's not going to try anything here."

A rational person wouldn't. But the stalker was beyond rational thought. He would take any opportunity to get to the object of his obsession—to Teddie.

Chapter 14

Teddie opened her mouth to scream, but her throat was so raw from all the smoke she'd inhaled that she barely managed a croak. Before she could try again, a latex-gloved hand pressed tightly over her mouth. While she tried again to scream, no sound made it out. It just burned in the back of her sore throat.

She struggled beneath the hand pressed over her face, but the man held her head down, pushing it into the pillows. His other hand encircled her throat in a tight vise, and he squeezed, cutting off her breath as well as her voice.

She reached up and clawed at his arms, trying to get him to release his hold on her so she could breathe. But either she was still too weak to fight him, or he was just too strong.

Her heart hammered in her chest as fear overwhelmed

her. Panic pressed on her lungs, stealing away the last of the breath in them. He was cutting off her oxygen.

She stared up into his face. But the gauzy mask covered most of it. All she could see were his eyes.

Had she ever seen those eyes, this man, before?

His eyes were dark, though not the deep, velvety chocolate of Manny's eyes. Just dark and cold—so cold. If anyone had ever looked at her the way this man was looking at her, she would have remembered it. She would have remembered that madness and hatred. It would have haunted her, just as he'd haunted her all these months since he'd sent her that first threatening note.

She rallied her strength. He was *not* going to beat her. At the moment she might not be physically strong, but she had always been emotionally strong. Growing up she'd had to fight hard to help her mother keep a roof over their heads and food in their bellies. She would fight now—for her life.

Because she could feel her life slipping away from her as she struggled for air. Digging deep with her nails, she clawed harder at his arms. Then she reached up for that mask, trying to tear it from his face. If she was going to die, she damn well wanted to know who was killing her—and why.

What had she ever done to him?

But he pulled back enough that she couldn't reach his face. His arms were longer than hers. And as his hand tightened even more around her throat, her vision began to blur. She could barely see him at all anymore as consciousness started to slip away from her. She was going to die—without ever learning who wanted her dead and why.

* * *

The trooper had given Manny the room number where he'd left Teddie. But he wasn't sure he would reach it in time. He knew—he just *knew*—that the stalker had already beaten him there. The hospital building was old and laid out like a maze, wings added on as the need had risen for more departments.

He ran down the corridors, narrowly dodging patients and medical staff. But he felt like he wasn't running fast enough, like he was caught in quicksand. Even as he was getting closer, she was slipping away from him.

Finally he turned the corner to the wing where she should be—if she were still here. He crashed through the door to find someone leaning over her.

The scrubs, the hat, the mask…the disguise was complete. But he knew it was only a disguise. He hurled himself at the guy, knocking him off the bed. They rolled across the floor and slammed into the wall. Manny grunted but the man made no sound at all. His arms and fists flailed, striking out at Manny. Then he grabbed for Manny's holster, for his gun.

Manny surged back to his feet, then reached down for the other man. Like the stalker had been holding Teddie by the throat, Manny caught him and lifted him to his feet, holding him only by his throat. Then he squeezed.

He should have killed him when he had the chance back at the cabin because it might be too late now. There was no movement from the bed, not even a whimper. The only sound was the door from the hall bursting open again and Dane's labored breathing.

The sound distracted Manny for just a moment, and

he loosened his hold fractionally. The guy struck out, slamming both fists against Manny's arm so he broke free of his grasp. But he had nowhere to run, not with both Manny and Dane in the room. Except the window. He turned and hurled himself through it.

Manny cursed.

"I've got him," Dane said as he used his sleeve to knock out the jagged glass before he jumped through the frame behind the stalker.

Manny turned back toward the bed, where Teddie's body lay limply against the pillows. His hand shaking, he reached out to check for a pulse. Before he could touch her, though, her lashes fluttered as her eyes opened.

She gasped for breath.

"Are you okay?" he asked.

Hospital staff poured into the room, pushing him aside as they treated her. Was she going to be okay?

He wanted to ask one of them, but he didn't want to interrupt. Trying to stay out of their way, he stepped into the hall, but he held the door open, leaning his back against it. He couldn't let her out of his sight. He never should have let her out of his sight.

But he struggled to see her now with so many hospital staff members hovering around her bed. "Sir!" a voice called out. He turned to see a nurse at a desk a short way down the hall, waving wildly at him. "Sir?" she called out. "Are you here with Ms. Plummer?"

He nodded.

"Her mother is on the phone," she called out. "She's hysterical."

Manny's stomach tightened into knots. He wasn't good with mothers. The girls he'd dated in high school had broken up with him right after they'd brought him home to meet their mothers. Because he was one of those Mannes men...

And then there had been the moms of the fellow Marines he'd lost. The ones he'd tried to comfort at their sons' funerals, only to have them cry harder.

No. He hadn't been kidding when he'd told Teddie that he wasn't good with mothers. His own mother barely tolerated his presence, probably because he reminded her too much of his father and brother.

"Please, sir," the nurse implored him. "She saw the news and she's scared to death."

So was he. He turned back to Teddie's room just as the staff stepped back. His heart plummeted to his stomach. Had they lost her?

But then they began to move the bed toward the doorway. He stepped back—out of their way—as they maneuvered it into the hall.

Were they taking her to surgery?

"Is she okay?" he asked anxiously.

Teddie held out a hand, which he grabbed as he walked alongside the rolling bed. There were calluses along her palms, and her hand was strong—not delicate like he would imagine a model's hands. Her nails were jagged with bits of skin and blood beneath them. She'd fought her stalker. She'd fought for her life.

Guilt overwhelmed him. She shouldn't have had to fight. She'd hired Payne Protection to take care of her. And they—*he*—had failed her.

"Are you okay?" he asked her.

"I'm—I'm okay," she whispered.

"If you hadn't gotten to her when you did..." one of the nurses murmured and shuddered.

He had nearly lost her. More than once.

He had never failed so dismally as a bodyguard until now, until it mattered most. Why did it matter most? Because this was his first assignment where he was primary or because the client was Teddie?

"Where are you taking her?" he asked.

"We're just moving her to a room without a broken window," the nurse explained.

Of course. He should have ordered that right away. Not that he expected the stalker to come back, unless it was on a gurney of his own. Dane would catch him. Wouldn't he?

Dane was hurt. He probably shouldn't have gone off alone after the stalker.

But while Dane was his friend, Teddie was his main responsibility. He wasn't going to leave her alone again. Not until he knew for certain that the stalker was caught and she was safe.

As they walked past the nurse's station, the older woman held out the phone toward him. "Sir…"

He caught the bed and held it to keep Teddie within sight. "Your mother's on the phone," he told her.

She shook her head and whispered, "She can't hear me like this…"

She didn't want to worry her mother.

"You talk to her," she urged him in a whisper.

If she didn't want to worry her mother, then she shouldn't have him talk to her. But he reluctantly accepted the receiver. "Mrs. Plummer?"

"Miss," the woman automatically corrected him. "Who is this?"

"Jordan Mannes," he replied.

"Who are you?" she demanded to know. Teddie had

said that her mother was feisty. He knew now that she hadn't been exaggerating.

"I'm your daughter's bodyguard."

"Not anymore," she said. "I just called your boss and fired the Payne Protection Agency. You haven't done anything to keep her safe."

He couldn't argue with her. And he couldn't justify his failures. How could he explain? *"I was sleeping with your daughter when the stalker set the cabin on fire"*?

He had no excuse for his lack of professionalism. Except that he would make certain it didn't happen again.

"I don't give a damn if you fired us, Miss Plummer," Manny said. "I am going to keep working this case until your daughter's stalker is either arrested or dead." At the moment, he would prefer dead.

"I—I…" the woman sputtered in his ear.

"Your daughter is fine now," he said, trying to assure himself as much as her. "She's safe, and I promise I will keep her that way."

He heard the breath she released in a ragged sigh. Then the bravado dissolved into sobs.

Why the hell did he always make mothers cry?

Cooper ran his hand over his short hair. Like Dane, he kept his as short as he had when he'd been a Marine. Dane…

"You're sure you're okay?" he asked his friend through the speaker on the cell phone he'd propped up on the conference room table. Cooper was alone in the room, staring at the muted television that kept running those photos of Teddie Plummer getting loaded into the back of an ambulance.

"Yeah, I'm fine. I'm just pissed," Dane admitted. "I let the bastard get the jump on me at the cabin. Then I wasn't able to catch him after he tried for her at the hospital."

"Your skull is fractured," Cooper reminded him.

Dane was lucky he'd been able to run after the stalker at all. Hell, he was damn lucky to be alive. But then, Cooper knew that Dane wasn't easy to kill. A lot of people had tried and failed.

"Are you really okay?" Cooper asked him.

"Yeah, yeah…"

"And Manny?"

"He's just pissed."

"I understand why," Cooper said. "This stalker is making me mad, too." He had nearly cost Cooper two of his best friends. If Manny hadn't escaped the fire…

"Manny's mad at himself," Dane said. "I've never seen him like this." He sounded concerned.

Cooper was, too. "Well, it may be a moot point now. Teddie's mother called earlier and fired us."

"Can she do that?" Nikki asked as she walked back into the conference room. "Her daughter hired us, right? Not her."

Cooper shrugged. "Teddie might want to fire us herself." He wouldn't blame her if she did.

Running his own franchise of Payne Protection wasn't as easy as Cooper had thought it would be. His very first client had tried firing him, too. If he had, he might have been alive today. But then Dane's fiancée wouldn't be. They had rescued her from the creep.

If Teddie Plummer would let them, the Payne Protection Agency would help her. Nikki had been working all night on the letters the stalker had sent, using them to track down his identity.

"I don't think she's going to fire Manny," Nikki said. "I saw the way she looked at him."

"Like what?" Cooper asked.

"The same way I look at Lars," Nikki said.

"What about Manny?" Cooper asked. "How was he looking at her?"

"Like he couldn't look away," Nikki said.

"I saw that, too," Dane agreed through the speaker. And he sounded every bit as worried about it as Cooper was.

Cooper groaned. No wonder Manny was pissed at himself. He'd let himself get distracted. If Teddie didn't follow through on her mother's wish to fire them, then Cooper would have to step in and remove Manny from this assignment.

His friend had been right about wanting to avoid any damsels in distress. Cooper never should have let him take the assignment in the first place. Now he had that sick, hollow feeling in his gut—almost a premonition—that something bad was going to happen.

That he was going to lose a friend…

Chapter 15

The late-morning sun barely shone through the thick trees around the ashes of Teddie's little cabin. Her sanctuary. It was gone. Somehow the fire had spread even to the storage shed. The Jeep stood inside the bare bones of the structure, a blackened shell of metal.

There was nothing left.

Teddie felt like that Jeep, burned out and hollow, as she stared at the destruction. She'd bought this place because she had thought she would be safe here. But she had nearly died in her *sanctuary*.

"We shouldn't have brought you here," Manny said. He and Dane had both gotten out of the SUV with her, but Dane stayed back, leaning against the passenger's side of it, his hand on his holster.

She had insisted on stopping by the cabin on their way to the private airstrip. She'd wanted to see if there was anything left of the life she'd wanted for herself. The quiet, the seclusion…

She felt none of that peace or serenity now. Instead she trembled as she remembered the fear of the night before, of nearly dying in the fire, only to be attacked later in the hospital. How had she inspired the hatred she'd seen in the eyes of the man who'd tried to kill her? She didn't even know him. What could she have done?

Manny slid his arm around her, but that only made her want to tremble more as she shivered in reaction to his closeness. Had they made love the night before?

It seemed as if it was only a dream now. Like a fantasy that had never happened. Had she only imagined the passion? The fire between them?

The sex hadn't lessened her attraction to him any. Her pulse quickened with his nearness. But the sex had been a mistake—one that had nearly gotten them both killed.

She had no business starting a relationship now—with anyone—until she was out of danger. And she wasn't the type to have sex without being in a relationship. She didn't know what had come over her the day before, why she had thrown herself at a man she barely knew.

She wished she could erase the memory as easily as the fire had erased the little cabin. But images kept replaying in her mind, images of the two of them kissing, touching…

She pulled away from him before she did something crazy again, like snuggle against his side as if they were a couple. Despite what had happened between them, they were still just a client and her bodyguard. They were not lovers. Teddie suspected she would never trust anyone enough to love him.

"You're right," she said. "There's nothing here any-more."

"The fire was set on the deck," Manny said. "The fire chief figured some gas-soaked rags and campfire wood were used to start it."

Anger coursed through her as she thought of the cabin being deliberately burned down. "I don't care how it started. I care *who* started it."

"You didn't get a good look at him in the hospital last night?" Dane asked the question.

She shook her head. "He was wearing a face mask and scrub hat." She shuddered. "I only saw his eyes." That had been full of such hatred and madness.

"You didn't recognize his eyes?" Manny asked.

"No, I didn't."

"But you must know him," he persisted. "Other-wise, why would he have bothered with the disguise?"

"So no one else would be able to identify him," she suggested.

She couldn't believe that this person—capable of such violence—was someone she knew. Sure, she'd trusted the wrong people before. But those people had sold her out for money and their own fifteen minutes of fame. While they had hurt her, they hadn't tried to kill her or anyone else.

Manny tilted his head. "I'm not so sure that was his reason for the disguise," he said. "It's not like there were any security cameras in that hospital."

"Too damn bad," Dane muttered.

"Too damn old," Manny said.

They probably hadn't ever needed security cameras before she'd moved to the area. The stalker hadn't just disrupted her life but the lives of everyone else with whom she came into contact.

Mama...

She'd been so upset. Teddie had been able to talk to her that morning when her throat had felt better. Mama had been upset about the fire, about Payne Protection, but mostly about Jordan Mannes.

"Are you sure you're safe with him?"

And for the first time in her thirty years, Teddie had lied to her mother. *"Yes, I'm safe with him."*

But she wasn't safe. While she trusted him with her life, she couldn't trust him with her heart. She was certain if she did, he would break it. He had already made it clear to her that he had no intention of ever having a serious relationship. Maybe that was why she'd had sex with him—because she'd known that was all he could ever give her.

And she'd been lonely enough to accept that then. But when she'd nearly died, she'd realized that she needed to protect herself. She couldn't completely trust anyone. "I didn't recognize him," she said.

Lately she hadn't recognized herself—at least, she hadn't recognized the woman who'd thrown herself at her bodyguard.

"I don't know him. I don't know why he would have done this." She gestured toward the destruction.

"I'm sorry," Manny said as if it was his fault. "I know you lost a lot."

She wasn't worried about the material things she had lost. It was the other things she'd lost that she mourned, like her peace and her peace of mind.

"You must have had insurance, right?" Dane asked, leaning against the SUV.

"I hadn't had time to find an agent up here," she admitted. "So, no…"

Dane cursed.

And she smiled. Years ago it would have bothered her what she'd lost. She and her mother had always had so little. But not now.

Manny must have realized the same thing. "I think she can afford this, Dane. She's a supermodel."

"I can afford this loss now," she agreed. "But there was a time losing anything would have devastated me. I grew up with nothing."

And then all she'd ever wanted was money because she'd thought that would give her peace and peace of mind. Once she didn't have to worry about keeping a roof over her head or food on the table, she would feel secure. And for a while she had.

Until those letters had started coming.

She shuddered. "At least the stalker's letters are gone, too."

Ashes like the rest of the cabin.

Manny shook his head. "Nikki took the folder with her when she left yesterday," he told her. "She's investigating them."

Teddie hadn't even noticed her taking the folder. She'd spent yesterday trying to avoid thinking about it and about her stalker. She had been totally focused on Manny instead.

Now she felt his focus, his concern, on her.

"We need to get out of here," he said with a slight shudder as if he'd gotten a chill. Or a creepy feeling like they were being watched?

Was *he* out there?

Of course he was. Wherever she was, her stalker

was never far behind. She was beginning to think that the only time she would ever escape him would be when he finally succeeded in killing her.

Teddie had been so quiet since they'd left the ashes of her cabin. Manny kept glancing over at her even as he checked the plane, making sure they were ready for takeoff. He'd double-checked everything on the outside. Now he examined the control panel.

Cole's Cessna was new, though, and quite safe, unlike the crop duster he'd flown up.

"Are you a nervous flier?" he asked her, and he was grateful again that Cole had left the Cessna.

Dane was a nervous flier. That was why he'd chosen a seat in the back of the plane, leaving the front for her. Of course, for guys like Dane it wasn't so much about flying as about not having control. That was why Manny had wanted to learn to fly himself.

Manny didn't figure Teddie for a control freak, though.

She shivered a little. "I wasn't nervous about flying before."

"Before the stalker?" He hated how much that bastard had messed with her life.

"I just felt trapped, thinking he could be up there with me and I had no escape." Her breath shuddered out in a ragged sigh. "Now I feel like that even when I'm not on a plane. I feel trapped—like I can't escape him—no matter where I go or what I do."

Manny reached over and clasped her hand. "He can't get you up here. There's no sneaking on this plane with us on board. And our flying back to River City will buy us plenty of time before he can figure out where we went and how to get to you again. You're safe, Teddie."

"Yeah," Dane chimed in from the back seat. "I think Manny did hit him last night, too. While I couldn't find him, I found some blood drops on the ground. I think he was bleeding."

That didn't mean Manny had hit him with a bullet, though. He could have just cut himself jumping out of the hospital window. But Manny didn't correct his friend. Maybe Teddie would relax some if she thought her stalker was seriously wounded.

It would help Manny relax, too, if he really believed that. But the man had moved fast. If he had been hit, it couldn't have been more than a scratch.

Damn it.

Teddie tugged her hand from beneath his and knotted it with her other one in her lap. She was still tense and on edge. But she obviously didn't want his comfort. She'd pulled away from him at the cabin, too.

Apparently he wasn't the only one regretting that they'd crossed the line the night before. He regretted it because he'd been so distracted that the stalker had nearly killed his friend and them.

Why did she regret it?

Had she realized that a bodyguard was beneath a supermodel? That there was no way they could ever have more than a fling? Manny had accepted that long ago. He'd known she would never be more than a fantasy to him.

"We're going to catch him," Dane said from the back seat. He was usually the quiet one of their unit. But maybe flying made him nervous enough to talk.

Manny knew it didn't matter what he and Dane said.

They weren't going to ease Teddie's fears any. Maybe they had only added to them because she would think that they weren't being realistic, that they wouldn't be prepared for the stalker's next attack.

While Manny had told her that the guy wouldn't be able to track them down for a while, he had his doubts. Her stalker had followed them quickly to the UP. It was almost as if he was a few steps ahead of them instead of behind them.

No matter what she said, the guy had to be someone she knew, someone she trusted. She probably didn't want to face the fact that once again someone had betrayed her trust. Manny could relate. That was why he trusted only those with whom he'd served. He knew they wouldn't betray him.

He knew they wouldn't break his heart. He couldn't say the same of Teddie Plummer.

While he understood her reasons for pulling away from him, he couldn't deny the twinge of pain in his chest. She could hurt him, probably even more than her stalker could.

He had been so close to them, just on the other side of the hangar, readying his plane for takeoff as they readied theirs.

He knew where they were headed. Even if he hadn't sneaked a look at their flight manifest, he would have known. River City, the home base for the Payne Protection Agency. Because he knew they'd talked to someone at the airstrip about keeping an eye open for anyone following them or going to River City, he'd filed his flight manifest first.

His plane took off before theirs. And he would land

his in a city several miles north of River City. They would never suspect him, just like she had never suspected him.

As he climbed into the cockpit, he grimaced, pain cramping his wounded leg. That bastard had shot him. Fortunately, the bullet had gone straight through, but the wound still hurt like hell.

He reached into his pocket and pulled out the bottle of pills he'd stolen from the hospital along with the scrubs. He'd also found some thick bandages he'd duct-taped around his thigh. He could feel his jeans sticking to them, though, so he suspected he'd bled through the bandages and the duct tape already. He would have his revenge soon against that damn bodyguard, though.

And he would have Teddie soon, too.

Chapter 16

As the steel door closed behind them, Teddie released a breath she hadn't realized she'd been holding. Maybe she'd been holding it since the fire. Or since that first letter had arrived.

She just knew that she finally felt safe here—inside the walls of this brick-and-metal condo that the Payne Protection Agency called their safest safe house. Her stalker wouldn't be able to burn down this structure or break in. The security system was top-notch, and the building itself was fairly indestructible and surrounded by Payne Protection bodyguards.

To be fair, though, she'd also briefly felt safe in Manny's arms, safe enough that she'd fallen into a sleep so sound that she had barely awakened when the fire had started. Or maybe that was because she'd been so satiated from making love with him.

Her face heated as she thought of it, of being with him. Was it as incredible as she remembered it being? Or had she romanticized it because he'd saved her life over and over again?

It couldn't have been that amazing, could it? She'd never felt that way before—with anyone. She had never felt so much pleasure.

"Thank you," she murmured.

Manny's dark brows arched in surprise over his dark eyes. "For what?"

She released a ragged breath of relief. "For making me feel safe again."

He nodded. "Good. That's why we brought you here. That's why we should have brought you here right away." A muscle twitched along his jaw.

He was obviously beating himself up for going along with Nikki Payne's decoy plan to draw out the stalker. Even if Nikki had looked exactly like Teddie, she doubted the plan would have worked. The stalker seemed to know her way too well. Could it be someone she knew, as Manny thought?

No. She'd been face-to-face with him as he had tried to choke the life from her. And she hadn't recognized anything in his eyes but madness. He was crazy.

But he wasn't here. He wouldn't be able to get to her in this condo like he had in the hospital. He wouldn't be able to hurt her here.

"I didn't think I could feel safe," she said, "not with him still out there." And she knew that he was. If Manny had shot him, he wouldn't have been as strong as he'd been in the hospital. No. If he was injured, it wasn't badly—not enough to stop him—probably only enough to make him more determined to hurt Manny and her. She shivered.

"We'll get him," he assured her, and he sounded as determined as the stalker had been. So she couldn't doubt that he would get him. Eventually.

She just wondered at what cost. How many of the other bodyguards might be hurt because of her? And how badly would Manny get hurt?

This was the job he had chosen, though. The life he wanted to live. One of danger. One in which it was better for him to be single, because if he ever had a family, there would probably be a day when he wouldn't be able to return to his wife and kids. Teddie had already been abandoned once, before she'd ever been born. She didn't want to risk that again.

His phone vibrated inside his jeans pocket, drawing her attention to his butt. The man was too damn good-looking. It wasn't fair. But even if she took the risk and fell for him, she had no guarantee he would return her feelings. She needed to remember that he was just doing his job. That was all she was to him—an assignment.

He pulled out the phone and glanced at the text on the screen. "Cooper wants to see me," he said.

"Cooper?"

"Cooper Payne," he said. "My boss."

"Oh, that's right." Cooper was the one she'd talked to when she'd hired the Payne Protection Agency. She waited for Manny to press a button and make a call.

But instead he headed toward the door.

And panic struck, stealing the breath from her still-achy lungs. "Where are you going?"

"I have to go in to the office," he said. His brow

furrowed slightly. He repeated slowly, "Cooper wants to *see* me."

"Can't he come here?" she asked.

Manny shook his head. "I don't think he can say what he wants to say to me in front of a client."

"What?" she asked, indignant on his behalf. "Do you think he's going to yell at you?"

He snorted. "Well, yeah…"

"Why?"

"Because I have it coming," he said. "You could have died last night—more than once."

"But I didn't," she said. "Because of you. You saved my life." He'd done that by more than just protecting her from the stalker. He'd saved her life when they'd made love because she'd felt something besides fear again.

She knew it was a bad idea. But she wanted to feel like that again. She wanted passion and pleasure without worrying about the consequences, without worrying about her heart getting broken.

He must have seen it in her face—the desire, the need—because he backed toward the door. And this time he was the one who looked scared. "Teddie…"

She was used to working for what she wanted. And she wanted Manny. She followed him until he stopped, his back pressed against that steel door. Then she pressed herself against him, stretching up his body to kiss his lips.

His breath escaped in a groan and her name. "Teddie…" Then he kissed her back.

And she felt it again, the passion that drove her wild. She tugged at his clothes, desperate to be close to him like they'd been that night. Skin to skin.

But he caught her shoulders and gently pushed her back. "Teddie, I—I can't do this."

Passion had already warmed her face, but now it burned with embarrassment. "I—I'm sorry…"

What was it about this man that made her lose all common sense and control? She had never thrown herself at anyone before him. But then, she'd never wanted anyone the way she wanted Jordan Mannes.

She stepped back from him and stared down at the floor, unable to meet his gaze. Maybe despite all of her denials she had become one of those spoiled celebrities used to getting her own way. Because she sure as hell couldn't handle this rejection.

It caused a pang in her chest that had nothing to do with panic or fear. Or maybe it had everything to do with that—because she was scared of what she was beginning to feel for a man who'd made it clear he had no intention of ever having a relationship with anyone.

She heard something strike the door and glanced up to see his palm pressed against it. Then he growled, "Damn it…" and whirled away from the door.

Seconds later he swept her up in his arms and carried her across the living room and through the doorway into another room. When she bounced down onto a mattress, she realized it was a bed.

"Damn you," he cursed her as he stripped off his holster and then his clothes.

Maybe she should have been insulted, but a giggle slipped out. He looked so angry, but she knew why. He had lost control. And for a man like him, a man who piloted his own planes, control was everything.

He wouldn't lose it if she didn't affect him in the same way he affected her. And damn, how he affected her. Wanting to be as naked as he was, she quickly stripped off all of her own clothes, tossing them down beside the bed.

His pupils dilated so his eyes were nearly black with desire. "I promised myself I wouldn't let you distract me again," he said. "The last time…" He shuddered.

"That wasn't your fault," she said. "The stalker would have set that fire anyway." Even if they hadn't been in bed together.

But he shook his head. "Not if I'd been keeping lookout instead of…"

"Dane was keeping lookout," she reminded him. "And now there are others outside, watching the condo." She repeated his words back to him. "I'm safe here."

But he shook his head again as he stared down at her lying naked on the bed. "You're not safe at all, Teddie Plummer. You're the most dangerous woman I've ever met." Then he followed her down onto the mattress, pressing his hard, tense body against hers.

She touched him everywhere, skimming her hands over his rippling muscles. As she touched him, he touched her—first just lips to lips. He kissed her gently, then more passionately, his tongue sliding into her mouth.

She ached for him to fill her, so she rubbed her hips against his straining erection. He groaned into her mouth. But he didn't take her with the fury she needed him to. Instead he moved his mouth down her body. He kissed her breasts, teasing the nipples with his lips and then his tongue.

She cried out as sensations raced through her. How could the man make her come just by touching her breasts?

"You are so damn responsive," he murmured.

But it wasn't enough. She needed all of him. She moved her hands between them, over his chest and washboard stomach to his erection. But he pulled back before she could stroke her fingers down the length of him.

Then she heard the tear of plastic as he ripped open a condom packet. This time he let her take it from him and roll it over his shaft. Her hand trembled as his flesh rippled beneath her fingers. She had never wanted anyone more than she wanted him. So she pushed him back on the bed and straddled him, sliding him inside her.

Like before, he filled that emptiness and eased that ache inside her. But as she moved, the tension increased, driving her out of her mind as release just eluded her.

He groaned and grasped her hips in his big hands. He moved her so that he slid a little deeper. She arched and cried out as sensations raced through her. But it still wasn't enough. She needed more.

His hands skimmed up from her hips to her breasts. He teased her nipples as he thrust up from the mattress. They moved in a frenzy.

Teddie felt as if she was losing her mind. She was so close to madness. Tension coiled tightly inside her, from her nipples to her core. Then her body convulsed, and she shuddered as she came.

He thrust his hips up and groaned, joining her in ecstasy. Panting for breath, he murmured again, "Damn you…"

She smiled, too satiated to be offended. She lifted herself off him and collapsed onto the bed in a tangle of sheets and limp limbs. She felt the mattress shift as he got up. Figuring he'd come back and wrap her in his arms like he had the night of the fire, she closed her eyes and waited for him. And drifted off to sleep.

Manny avoided the rearview mirror. He couldn't risk catching a glimpse of himself. He was too disgusted. Not only had he given in once again to his desire for the client, but he had also left her lying alone in bed after giving in to that desire. Of course, she wasn't completely alone. Payne Protection bodyguards surrounded the condo.

Cooper had called in reinforcements from Logan's team and from his brother Parker's. Parker's former vice cops with their thick beards and rough appearances fit in well in the abandoned industrial area of River City where the condo had been converted from an old warehouse. Nobody would suspect them of being hired security, just like their former targets hadn't suspected they were cops. And Logan's team had the most experienced of the bodyguards—the ones who'd saved the most lives already.

With all that protection, nobody would get to Teddie.

But she had gotten to Manny in a way nobody else ever had—which proved his judgment was every bit as bad as that of the other Mannes men. Not that Teddie would ever ask him to commit a crime.

But his desire for her had affected what had always been most important to him: his commitment to a mission. He had never let himself get distracted before. Despite his sometimes big mouth, he had never been a risk to the success of a mission before, either.

He had already nearly failed this mission when Dane had been hurt, when the cabin had burned and when the stalker had gotten to Teddie in the hospital. He had promised her mother, and himself, that he would keep her safe until he caught her stalker.

He understood now that she would be safer without him near her. Because his desire for her distracted him.

Cooper was no doubt going to remove him from the assignment. And this time Manny would not argue with his boss. It would be safer for Teddie and for him if someone else protected her.

But he wouldn't break his promise to her mother. He would make certain that she stayed safe—with other bodyguards—and he would make damn sure her stalker was caught.

Metal crunched, and his head snapped forward as someone struck the rear of the Payne Protection SUV he drove. He glanced to the rearview mirror that he had been avoiding. Maybe someone had just accidentally struck him. Maybe, in his reluctance to face his boss, he hadn't been driving the speed limit. But when he looked into the mirror, he could see the driver of the truck—and the man was wearing a ski mask very much like the one Manny had found at the stalker's campsite.

He cursed and pressed hard on the accelerator. But the truck engine revved as the driver sped up to close the distance between them again. The bumpers connected, and this time Manny was ready for the impact. It barely jostled him.

He jerked the wheel, taking a sharp turn. The truck nearly missed it, jumping the curb and going over the sidewalk to follow him. A street vendor's cart flew, debris hitting the truck windshield. But still the truck kept coming.

As determined as the stalker had been to get to Teddie, he seemed just as determined to get to Manny now. Manny reached for his cell, but the pocket where he always kept it was empty. He'd left his phone at the condo, so he couldn't call for backup. He would have to take out the stalker on his own.

Or die trying…

Nikki Payne had always envied her mother's special ability to just *know* things. And probably one of the things she'd resented most when her illegitimate brother Nick came to town was that he had that same special ability. And he wasn't even Penny Payne's son.

Well, he was now, because Penny had a way of adopting everyone she met. But Nikki had always wished she could just *know* things, too.

As she watched her brother Cooper grapple with his new ability, she wasn't so envious anymore. At the head of the conference table, he looked tense and miserable and scared.

"What is it?" she asked.

"Manny's late," he said.

"He left late," she reminded him. From his post outside the condo door, Cole had let the boss know when Manny had finally exited the safe house.

It had taken him a while to leave Teddie. Nikki was actually a little surprised and disappointed that he had. She'd thought he was falling for the supermodel.

Maybe that was why he'd left. He was running scared from his feelings for Teddie. Nikki understood that fear very well.

Not too long ago she had run from her feelings for his friend Lars. But she hadn't been able to run fast or far enough to escape love, and she suspected neither would Manny.

Under the conference room table, she reached for her fiancé, sliding her hand over his muscular thigh. Lars glanced over at her, his pale blue eyes bright with desire and love.

She wasn't afraid anymore. She trusted Lars more than anyone else in the world, even her mother. He was a man of honor and integrity, and worthy of her trust.

From what she'd learned about Teddie Plummer, she appeared to be worthy of Manny's trust, as well. Nikki had found no reason for anyone to target the supermodel, who was believed to be as beautiful on the inside as she was on the outside.

Which meant their suspect could be anyone…

After her plan had failed, Nikki had worked hard to redeem herself. Using the photos, she'd managed to compile a list of possible suspects. But she didn't think that was the only reason Cooper had called this meeting.

He cursed.

"What is it?" she asked.

"I just have a bad feeling," he murmured, confirming her suspicion that he was getting premonitions just like their mother did. And it was obviously making him miserable. "I think something has happened to Manny."

Lars snorted. "Yeah, he's falling for a supermodel."

Cooper shook his head. "No, I think…" He cursed again and picked up his cell phone. He punched a contact and the sound of ringing emanated from his speaker.

But Manny didn't answer the call. The hello that echoed throughout the conference room was, albeit throaty and faint, feminine.

"Miss Plummer?" Cooper asked.

"Y-yes," she replied. She sounded disoriented, like she had just awakened. Had she been sleeping alone?

"Sorry," he said. "I was trying to reach Manny."

She hesitated for a moment as if she was looking for him before she murmured, "He's not here. He must have forgotten his phone."

Nikki and Lars exchanged a pointed glance. Manny had forgotten his cell phone in the bedroom? She hadn't been wrong about the attraction she'd noticed between the supermodel and her bodyguard. She wasn't surprised that they'd acted on that attraction. There was something about being in danger that was almost like an aphrodisiac. Lucky for her, she and Lars were bodyguards.

"That's fine," Cooper said.

But Teddie must have realized it wasn't because her voice was sharp when she asked, "Isn't he there with you?"

"No…"

"Then where is he?"

And finally Nikki felt it, too. Her brother's bad feeling overwhelmed her. Something had happened to Manny. The stalker must have realized he was never going to get to Teddie unless he got rid of her overprotective bodyguard first.

"We'll find him," Cooper assured their client. But he didn't sound hopeful.

And Nikki knew why. Her brother didn't expect to find his friend alive.

Chapter 17

As a model, Teddie was used to quick changes of clothes. But she had never dressed as quickly as she had after Cooper Payne had disconnected his call to Manny's cell phone. Her hands trembled around the phone. It must have fallen out of his pocket when he'd pulled off his clothes.

So he was out there. Alone. Without a phone.

And he hadn't arrived yet at the Payne Protection Agency. Cooper must have been worried about Manny. Why else would he have called?

And now Teddie was worried. She ran out of the bedroom, across the hardwood floor of the open living area to that steel door. She pulled at the knob, but it didn't turn. There was no lock on the handle, just a panel next to the door.

She needed a code to open the door?

Just a short while ago she had felt safe inside the condo. But that had been when Manny was inside it with her. Now she felt trapped. Panic pressing on her lungs, she pounded on the door and called, "Let me out!"

Her throat hurt as she yelled. The smoke from the fire and the stalker strangling her had done damage. But she didn't care. She yelled louder, her voice cracking with pain and panic. "Let me out!"

The knob rattled before it turned and the door opened. But it wasn't Manny standing on the other side like she had hoped. Cole Bentler stared down at her, his blue eyes wide with surprise. "What's wrong?" he asked.

"You tell me," she said. "Where's Manny?"

"Cooper called him to a meeting."

She held out Manny's cell phone. "Cooper called here because Manny hasn't shown up."

Cole sucked in a breath. If he'd been standing guard at the door, he knew when Manny had left. And he knew how long it would take to get to the Payne Protection office. "Is this Manny's phone?" he asked.

She nodded as heat rushed toward her face. "He must have dropped it."

Cole probably suspected how. But all she saw on his face was concern for his friend. Unless he was concerned about Manny getting involved with her.

At the moment Teddie was concerned, too. "Where could he be?"

Cole shrugged and suggested, "Maybe he stopped off at our place for a shower or change of clothes before going to the office."

That sounded reasonable. But then she remembered

how Cooper had sounded on the phone and she shook her head. "Your boss sounded scared."

Cole snorted. "Cooper? Scared?"

"Worried," she amended. She was the one who was scared, her heart beating fast.

Cole's blue eyes darkened to navy, and he murmured, "Damn it…"

"What is it?"

He shrugged. "The Payne family has this weird premonition thing…" He shook his head. "I'm sure there's nothing to it."

"But?"

"Naw, I'm sure Manny's fine," he said as if trying to convince himself. "What reason could anyone have for going after Manny?"

"To get to me," she said. She had put him in danger. And if her obsessed stalker had any idea how she was falling for her bodyguard, he would have another reason for wanting him dead. Jealousy…

Cole closed his eyes and cursed again. "I'll get someone else to watch the door and I'll go find him."

Before he could turn and walk away, she grasped his arm. "I'm going with you."

"Absolutely not."

But she pushed her way past him. "You can't hold me here against my will," she pointed out. "And I don't want to be here."

Not without Manny.

"This is a bad idea," Cole warned her.

She'd had quite a few of those lately. Making love with Manny…

If something had happened to him, it was her fault. She had made him a target for the stalker.

"You're safe in the condo," Cole persisted. "You need to stay here with the security system and all the perimeter bodyguards. Nobody can get to you here."

She shook her head. "I won't stay here." She didn't care how safe it was. "I want to go with you and find Manny."

"I don't know where to look for him," Cole warned her.

"Your place," she said. "And the route to Payne Protection."

His eyes narrowed as he speculatively studied her face. Maybe he'd bought into the stereotype that models were stupid. The few models she'd met who had fit that stereotype hadn't lasted long in the fashion business. They hadn't had what it took to survive. Brains were as necessary as beauty in her business.

Just like brains were as necessary as brawn to survive as a bodyguard. Manny was every bit as smart as he was muscular. He'd outmaneuvered the stalker more than once. Hopefully he had managed this time, as well. Because Teddie had the feeling his boss was right to be worried and so was his friend.

The stalker had gone after Manny.

Manny had played chicken many times before. He had started as a kid, riding his bike head-on toward his brother. His brother had always veered first. Maybe that had just been because he was older and he hadn't wanted to hurt Manny. But the other people with whom he'd played chicken hadn't cared whether or not they'd hurt him. They'd been trying to protect themselves when they'd veered off first. Because they must have sensed there was no way he was going to veer.

But Manny should have known better than to play chicken with a lunatic. He'd figured it was the only way to stop the crazy bastard. The problem was that the stalker wasn't the only one who was going to get hurt.

Manny had led him away from the city limits, though, to avoid anyone else getting caught between the SUV and the truck. He'd driven fast, but not so fast that he would lose him, toward the more rural area and winding roads closer to the Lake Michigan shoreline.

He lost him once, on one of those sharp curves of road. But because he hadn't wanted the stalker to double back around to the condo, Manny had executed a dangerous U-turn. The stalker must have followed him from the condo.

How the hell had he known where it was?

Who was this guy that it almost seemed as if he had inside information on the Payne Protection Agency? Or was it just on Teddie?

The only person she'd talked to since he'd started protecting her had been her mother. So it didn't make sense how he always knew where she was.

Now Manny needed to know where the hell the stalker was. Then he saw the truck heading at him and breathed a sigh of relief. He hadn't doubled back. He was still intent on taking out Manny.

Manny just had to take him out first.

He could have tried shooting him. But driving as fast as they were, he needed both hands on the wheel. And at these speeds, it was too likely any bullet even Manny fired would miss. He couldn't take the risk of the stalker getting away again—not like he had so many times before.

Manny revved his engine as he headed straight toward the truck. The Payne Protection SUVs were special, with reinforced frames and metal. Because the bodyguards had been in so many crashes previously, their vehicles had been made to withstand them better now.

But Manny wasn't sure the SUVs had been tested in a head-on collision—until now. Because everyone else had always veered off, Manny had never been tested in a head-on collision, either. What was the trick to absorbing the impact?

Being relaxed?

He blew out a breath and let himself go limp even as he pushed harder on the accelerator. With resolve he stared straight ahead through the windshield. If only the guy would take off that damn mask.

Even now he hung on to his disguise.

And in those last seconds before impact, Manny closed his eyes. Maybe it was instinct. Maybe it was because even though this guy had terrorized Teddie, Manny didn't want to watch him die.

Metal crunched as the vehicles collided. The SUV spun around and around again, tires squealing even though Manny hadn't applied the brakes. The axles must have broken because he had no control over the steering. The wheel spun loosely in his hands as the SUV spun around the road, then careened off and into the trees lining it.

The second impact must have been what got him. Despite all the airbags springing out of the steering wheel and the doors, Manny hit his head on something.

And everything went black.

For just a moment, though, because Manny fought his way back to consciousness. Teddie needed him. She needed him to stop her stalker and give her back her life—whatever life she wanted to live now.

Manny dragged his eyes open and stared around him. The windows looked like spiderwebs, shattered but intact. He couldn't see through them, though. He needed to see if the stalker was coming for him. Or if Manny had finally stopped him for good.

As a precaution he drew his weapon. Then he reached for the door handle. But the door was jammed against a tree. He couldn't escape. So he moved toward the dash instead and kicked out the shattered glass. He climbed over the crumpled hood and hissing engine until his feet hit the ground.

His legs were a little shaky but held his weight. Gun drawn, he swept the barrel around the area. A man rolled over from where he lay on the side of the street, next to the smashed-up truck.

"Don't move!" Manny shouted at him. But he kind of hoped he would so that he would have a reason to shoot him. How the hell had the guy survived the crash?

Only the back of the truck was recognizable, the box the only thing intact.

"Don't shoot," the man implored him. He was an elderly man—with white hair and a small, almost stooped build. He moved slowly, lurching to his feet.

There was no way in hell that this man had overpowered and outrun Dane.

Manny swept his barrel toward the truck. "Where is he? Where's that driver?"

"I was behind you guys," the older man said. "I saw him jump out right before the crash, and I just managed not to hit him. Once he got up, he opened my door and pulled me out. He stole my car."

Manny cursed. The son of a bitch had cheated in chicken. He had jumped out before the impact. If only Manny hadn't closed his eyes…

He cursed himself now.

"Do you have a phone?" he asked—hopefully.

He needed to warn the others. The stalker had nearly taken him out. Hell, he probably thought that he had. Now he had to be headed straight for Teddie.

If Manny wasn't dead, he would probably kill Cole for letting Teddie out of the safety of the condo. But short of tying her up, he wasn't sure how he would have been able to get her to stay.

They'd already been to the attic apartment he shared with Manny. She had seemed unusually interested in where Manny lived. Even though it had been immediately apparent that he wasn't there, she had looked around at the few possessions Manny owned, at the few mementos he'd kept. She'd run her fingertips over the dog tags he'd left sitting on the bureau in his room. She'd also touched the pillow on his unmade bed.

The place, with its galley kitchen and small living room, probably hadn't looked like much to her. Cole could have afforded better. But Manny couldn't, not with as much money as he sent home to help his mother every month. Cole wondered why he bothered since she didn't seem to appreciate it much. She never called or checked on him. She didn't worry about him like his unit worried. Since Cole hadn't wanted to hurt Manny's pride, he had found a place they could rent that his friend could easily afford.

He and Teddie were heading toward the offices of the Payne Protection Agency now. Cole glanced over to the passenger's seat of the SUV, where Teddie had knotted her fingers together in her lap.

"You're really worried," he mused.

"Aren't you?" she asked.

He was. But he didn't want her to know that. "Manny's tough," he told her. "He's survived far worse than whatever your stalker might dish out."

She nodded. But he could tell she was not reassured.

"He will be fine," Cole insisted. This was Manny, after all. "Yeah, he'll be fine."

And as if on cue, Cole's cell vibrated in his pocket. He pulled it out and hit Accept and Speaker. "Cooper, we couldn't find him."

"He just called in," Cooper said. "He's okay. But the stalker got away. He thinks he's coming after Teddie. He wanted to make sure she's safe in the condo."

A pang of guilt struck Cole. "She's with me," he replied.

"I know," Cooper said. "You took her out of the condo, so you better make damn certain she stays safe."

Or Manny would kill him.

"We're close to the office," Cole assured him. "We'll be there soon."

"Good," Cooper said. "Then we can all share what we know and see if we can figure out this guy's identity." He disconnected the call.

"So Manny's okay," Teddie said on a shuddery breath of relief.

Cole nodded. "See, I told you he's tough." Tougher even than Cole had realized, since Manny had survived another run-in with her stalker. The guy had nearly killed Dane, and Dane was the most invincible one of them all.

But Manny had extra motivation to stay alive now. Teddie. He was determined to keep her safe, and Cole doubted it was just because she was a client. She was more to Manny. And because of that, Cole never should have let her leave the safety of the condo. Manny might never forgive him if something happened to her.

Cole kept an eye on the rearview mirror, watching for anyone tailing them. But he'd been careful. Still, he breathed his own sigh of relief as he pulled the SUV into the parking lot of the Payne Protection Agency. He had made it to the office without losing their client. After shutting off the engine, he stepped out.

But as he walked around the SUV to her side of the vehicle, something—like a baseball bat—struck him across the backs of his knees, knocking his legs from beneath him. He fell, hitting the pavement hard. His head bounced off the asphalt and black spots blurred his vision.

From where he lay, he couldn't see anything. He could only hear Teddie's scream.

Yeah, Manny was going to kill him.

Chapter 18

If only she'd moved faster...

Teddie might have been able to warn Cole about the man who'd sprung from the shadows between two SUVs. She might have been able to lock her door to stop him from grabbing her and dragging her from the SUV.

She'd placed her hand on the door, but instinct had her opening it to rush to Cole's aid. He was down. The man in the mask had whacked him hard with a bat. She had no idea how badly Cole was hurt.

Ignoring the pain of her still-sore throat, she screamed again, trying to draw attention. They were so close to the brick building with the sign on the side of it for The Payne Protection Agency. She kicked and swung out, fighting off Cole's attacker.

Her stalker.

He wore a mask again, one of those ski masks that

hid his entire head except for his eyes. But she couldn't see his eyes. Her back was to him, his arms wrapped around her torso as he dragged her toward a van parked near the parking-lot exit. He carried her through the open side door and pulled it closed behind him. Dropping her onto the bare metal floor, he jumped into the driver's seat and gunned the engine.

As he careened out of the lot, Teddie rolled across the back and struck the metal side of the cargo van. Pain radiated from her elbow up her arm. Her hand went numb, but she shook it off. She had to escape now before he got her off somewhere alone.

Because she knew then she would have no chance of escaping. No chance for survival.

She had to get away. Now.

But the van took another sharp turn and she rolled again. This time she caught herself against the metal side and used it to get to her feet. This was the side of the van with the door, and her hands gripped the handle.

She jerked it open and stared down at the asphalt. The van was moving fast. But she had no choice. If she didn't get away now, she wouldn't have another chance. Before she could jump, a hand caught her arm. The van slowed and swerved as the driver twisted in his seat to hold on to her.

He was strong, his fingers squeezing her arm painfully. He was nearly as desperate to hang on to her as she was to escape him. But with his attention divided between gripping her and driving, she was able to jerk free.

And as she did, she tumbled out of the van. Just like she'd rolled across the cargo area of the van, she rolled across the street. The asphalt tore at her clothes and scraped her hands and her cheek. She cried out at the pain.

Brakes and tires squealed as the van abruptly stopped in the middle of the road. Metal creaked as the driver's door opened. He was coming after her again.

Her hands stinging and raw from the scrapes, she pushed herself to her feet and took off running. She had outrun him once—in the park in New York. But he had caught her in the woods up north.

She couldn't let him catch her this time.

Ignoring the burning feeling in her legs, she ran as fast as she could. She headed across a parking lot toward a row of tall buildings. She could hear footsteps pounding against the ground behind her as he pursued her. She could also hear horns honking as other drivers protested his leaving the van in the middle of the street.

Panting for breath, lungs burning like her legs, she continued to run. She couldn't stop now. She couldn't give up. She dodged between two tall brick buildings, hoping she'd found an alley. But another building blocked the end of it. She was trapped.

If she turned around, he would catch her on the way back out. So she needed to hide. Maybe he wouldn't find her. She crawled into a small space between a rusted metal Dumpster and a brick wall. Her back pressed against the building and her breasts pushed against the metal as she continued to pant for breath.

The air was putrid near the Dumpster, thick with the scent of rotting food and urine. She grimaced and tried not to breathe now. She couldn't give away her location.

Because she was no longer alone.

She could hear the scrape of shoes against the asphalt. He must have seen where she'd run. But maybe he wouldn't be able to see where she was hiding. The tall buildings cast deep shadows in the alley, so there was little light. Now there was even less as a dark shadow fell across her.

Then a big hand touched her arm. She held on to the rusted metal of the Dumpster, so he wouldn't be able to drag her from her hiding place—like he had from the SUV.

She didn't know if anyone, in the buildings or on the street, would be able to hear her, but she screamed. Straining her still-injured lungs and throat, she screamed as loudly as she could. But she doubted, even if anyone heard her, that help would arrive in time to save her.

Her scream rang in Manny's ears as he reached out for her again. She had tugged free of his light grip on her arm.

"Shh, it's okay," he said, her fear causing a twinge of pain in his heart. He hated seeing her like this, so full of terror. He hated feeling it nearly as much, and he had been so afraid for her. "He's gone."

She turned toward him, as much as she could in her hiding place, and her green eyes widened in surprise as she stared up at him. He pulled the Dumpster away from the wall, astonished that she had squeezed into such a narrow space.

Teddie scrambled out and threw her arms around his neck. He winced when she pressed against ribs he hadn't even realized he'd bruised until then. But he didn't care about the pain. He didn't give a damn about himself.

"Are you okay?" he asked, gently tipping her face

up to his. One of her cheeks was red and scraped, as were her arms and her knees through her torn jeans. Pride surged through him that she had fought so hard to escape her stalker.

But she shouldn't have had to fight. It was the Payne Protection Agency's job to keep her safe from harm. And once again they had failed her.

He should have ignored Cooper's order to come to the office. He should have kept the promise he'd made her mother that he would personally keep her safe until the stalker was caught. But he'd thought he could trust the others to protect her.

"Are you all right?" he asked again, anxiously.

She nodded. "Is Cole okay? The—the man came out of nowhere and hit him so hard."

"I didn't see Cole," he said. He hoped like hell his friend was all right. "I just saw you—running." But the stalker must have gotten the jump on Cole just like he had on Dane and on him, too. That was why Teddie never should have left the security of the condo.

"Why aren't you back at the safe house?" he asked. "Why the hell are you here?"

"Because of you," she murmured, pulling away from him.

He flinched again as if she'd squeezed his sore ribs. But she had actually stepped back and dropped her arms from around him.

"Cooper called your cell phone when you didn't show up at the office," she said. "You'd left it on the bedroom floor." Her face flushed, all of her skin turning as red as her scraped cheek.

That never should have happened. He shouldn't have crossed the line with a client once again, because once again he had risked both their lives. If he hadn't been so distracted because of making love with her again, he would have noticed the stalker following him.

And if they hadn't made love, he wouldn't have dropped his cell phone. He would have had it to call for backup. Fortunately, the elderly man whose vehicle the stalker had jacked had a cell phone on him.

"What happened to you?" she asked as her gaze ran over his face. "Are you okay?"

Manny jerked his head up and down in a quick nod. "Yeah, I'm fine. He tried running me off the road."

But Manny was the one who had caused the real wreck and had lost the stalker because of it. At least the elderly man had called the police right away, even before Manny had gotten out of the SUV. So they had arrived quickly, probably because they'd already had reports of the erratic driving, and they'd agreed to bring Manny back to the Payne Protection Agency, lights flashing.

He would have been too late if Teddie hadn't jumped from the van. From the passenger's seat of the police car, he'd seen her leap out. And his heart had leaped from his chest along with her. He'd seen her tumble and roll across the asphalt. He'd watched the stalker stop the van and run after her.

But when the stalker had heard the sirens, he'd stopped chasing after Teddie. Unfortunately, he'd disappeared inside a parking garage. The police officer had gone after him while Manny had run after Teddie.

Manny wasn't going to hold his breath hoping that the stalker would be caught in that parking garage. He was too good at escaping.

Too damn good…

They needed to catch him—needed to *stop* him—before he got Teddie or killed one of them. If he hadn't already.

He needed to check on Cole and make sure his friend was all right. And if he was, Manny would give him hell for not protecting Teddie.

Cooper looked around the conference room table, studying the faces of his team. That damn feeling he'd had…had been right. Something bad had happened.

But not just to Manny.

Cole should have gone to the hospital like Cooper had wanted when he'd found him lying in the parking lot a short while ago. Dark circles rimmed his eyes, and he looked like hell.

Dane didn't seem much better. He had still not recovered from his run-in with the stalker.

And Manny…

He didn't look like he'd just totaled one of the Payne Protection Agency SUVs. He had just a small bump near his temple.

No. What was most upsetting about Manny was that he looked like he was about to kill.

Cooper understood his friend's frustration. He was frustrated himself that this stalker kept eluding and hurting his team. Because of that, the assignment had gotten personal for him. He suspected it had gotten even more personal for Manny.

The dark-haired bodyguard sat close to the client, as if he needed to protect her even in the conference room of Payne Protection. Of course, she had just been abducted from the parking lot, so Manny was smart to be vigilant.

Teddie Plummer looked worse than Cole and Dane. A twinge of regret struck Cooper's heart that they had not done a better job of protecting her. Maybe that was why Manny appeared so angry and frustrated.

Or maybe what was bothering him most was the list of suspects Nikki had compiled on the board at the front of the room. If he had feelings for Teddie, like his friends suspected, then maybe it was bothering him to see pictures of her past boyfriends and old flames.

Not that she had many.

But Cooper could remember when his wife—although she'd just been a friend then—had been receiving threatening notes. He remembered the frustration and the helplessness he had felt. It had been personal to him then, like it was personal to Manny now.

Was his friend falling for their client?

Cooper hoped he wasn't, because he knew how loyal Manny was, how self-sacrificing.

If Manny had fallen for Teddie Plummer, he would do anything to protect her—kill or be killed.

Chapter 19

Teddie almost regretted now that she'd insisted on sitting in on this Payne Protection Agency meeting. Her life was laid out on one wall of the conference room. All those threatening letters had been pinned to a board along with pictures of several men.

Her face heated with embarrassment while her cheek throbbed from scraping the asphalt. "What is this?" she asked, gesturing at the pictures. "Why are they up there?"

"Because they're possible suspects," Nikki Payne said. She stood near the board. "I identified the men in your past who might have become obsessed with you."

A nervous chuckle slipped through her lips, and she shook her head. "That's not possible."

None of her previous relationships had ever been serious enough for anyone to harbor resentment against her for breaking up. There had never really been anything to break up beyond a few casual dates.

She hadn't even had much time for dating between work and classes and her mom. Or maybe those had just been excuses, so she hadn't had to risk her heart on a man she might not be able to trust.

Unable to sit down any longer with everyone dissecting her life, she stood up and joined Nikki at the board. Pointing at a photo, she said, "I never dated him." She shuddered at the thought. "He's my former manager."

"Former," Nikki said. "You fired him. He has every reason to be angry with you."

"No," Teddie said. "It wasn't like that. He wasn't mad at me. He agreed that it would be better to have someone else manage my career." It had become too much for him to handle along with his other clients.

"He willingly agreed to give up his percentage of all your future modeling jobs?" Cole asked, clearly skeptical.

"Yes," she said. "Ed Bowers is a nice guy. There is no way he would have sent me any of those." Her finger shook as she pointed at the desecrated photographs.

"What about him?" Manny asked. He'd joined her and Nikki at the board. He pointed to a photograph of a man who was so handsome he could have been a model; instead, he'd photographed them.

Heat rushed to Teddie's face again. "I don't know why Anthony Esch is up here."

"You dated him," Nikki said.

"How do you know that?" Teddie asked. The relationship—if a few casual and awkward dates could be called that—had been brief and kept private. Unlike all her fictitious relationships, it had never made the tabloids. Yet none of those rumored boyfriends had photos up there. "How do you know which relationships were real or just gossip?"

Nikki smiled. "I'm that good."

"So ol' Tony was a real boyfriend," Manny said. "What happened? Why did you dump him?"

"I didn't," Teddie said. "It was a mutual decision."

Manny arched a dark brow. He was as skeptical of this breakup as Cole had been of the agent one.

Teddie hated this—hated having to talk about herself. She'd bought that cabin so she didn't have to deal with reporters invading her privacy and firing questions at her. She hadn't realized she would have to deal with the same invasion of privacy when she hired the Payne Protection Agency. But because she wanted her stalker caught and her privacy back, she knew she had to answer their questions.

"We only went out a few times," she said. "It wasn't serious. We were both too busy." And despite working in the same industry, they'd had nothing in common and absolutely no chemistry. Despite how good-looking Anthony was, Teddie had never been attracted to him like she was Manny.

Manny studied the photograph. "It could be him. He's about the right size."

"So's Bowers," Dane said.

Teddie shook her head. "I told you, it can't be someone I know."

"Why not?" Manny asked. "You've already admitted that other people close to you have betrayed you."

She pointed at some of the other pictures. "He was an assistant who sold photos and info to the tabloids," she said. "But he has no reason to be angry with me." It was the other way around. "I only went out with this guy once, to a charity ball. Same with this guy." Frustration welled up inside her. "Nobody I know has any reason to stalk me. The stalker is not someone I know."

"It has to be someone you know," Manny persisted, "because he seems to know you. Very well."

She shook her head. "I—I would have recognized him." Touching her throat, she said, "I was staring up into his face when he was choking me."

"And he was wearing a mask," Manny reminded her. "He always wears a mask. He must think you will recognize him if he doesn't."

"Or he's worried that someone else will be able to identify him if he doesn't wear a disguise," Teddie said.

"That's true," Nikki agreed and asked her, "Who do you think could do this?"

Teddie sighed. "I wish I knew. I got other weird letters before, but none like these." She didn't even want to look at them.

"You have other letters?" Nikki asked. "Where are they?"

"I used to throw them out," she admitted. She hadn't taken them seriously then, not until these more disturbing ones started arriving. "But I might have a couple at my apartment in New York."

"We need those," Nikki said. "We need to see if these—" she gestured at the board "—are an escalation from those prior ones."

"Those were just weird fan letters," Teddie said. "Not threats." Some had been compliments. "They were bizarre but not scary."

"We need them," Cooper agreed. "Manny, you need to fly to New York and get them right away."

Manny shook his head. "I'm sticking with Teddie, and Teddie needs to go back to the condo and stay there."

After he'd found her in the alley, he'd wanted to bring her back there. But she'd insisted on sitting in on this meeting. She regretted that now—regretted how much she'd had to reveal about her life. Not that she'd really revealed it. Nikki had already seemed to know.

"Lars and Nikki will bring Teddie back to the condo," Cooper said. "And you'll fly out alone."

"Cole can fly out," Manny said. "I'll bring her back to the condo."

"Cole might have a concussion," Cooper said. "We're not going to risk it. You'll go." And his tone brooked no argument, reminding Teddie that this was his agency.

He was the boss.

Manny must have remembered that, as well, because he stopped arguing and turned toward the door.

But she couldn't let him just walk away. "You can't go!" she protested.

"Miss Plummer, Lars and Nikki will protect you," Cooper assured her.

"I know," she said. "But who will protect Manny if the stalker tries for him again?" He had nearly been run off the road, shot and burned up. The stalker seemed as obsessed with Manny as he was with her.

Was that just because Manny had been guarding her? Or was it because he somehow knew that she had developed feelings for her bodyguard and he was jealous?

No matter his reason, it was clear Manny was in just as much danger as she was—if not more.

Manny was pissed—for so many reasons. And his friend must have picked up on his anger, because Cole said, "I'm sorry."

"You're not the one who forced me to come here," Manny said and bitterly added, "Our boss's orders sent me here." To Teddie's apartment in New York City. He closed the door behind them and sucked in a breath at the view of the city through the floor-to-ceiling windows.

Cole sucked in a breath, as well. "Damn, this is some place."

The living room was probably five times bigger than the entire cabin her stalker had burned down. The ceiling was higher even than the peak of the A-frame. The floors were polished marble, and the furniture was high-end.

Manny's stomach lurched, and it had nothing to do with his frustration over not catching the stalker yet. He felt sick because he knew now—without a doubt—that Teddie would never want more than protection from him. Their lives were far too different. She might have grown up poor like he had, but she was used to luxury now. She wouldn't want to give up everything for which she had worked so hard to live the simple life she'd claimed she wanted.

And if she didn't want a simple life, she didn't want him. Sure, she had wanted him before, but she'd probably only been using sex with him as a distraction from the danger she'd been in for so long.

He couldn't blame her. He also couldn't help feeling

a little used and hurt. But he should have known better, should have known she was just a fantasy. And he should be grateful that during those wildly passionate moments, he'd had the chance to live out his fantasy.

But there was no chance of that fantasy becoming a lasting reality.

"Let's find these letters and get back to River City," Manny said. He hadn't wanted to leave her again, not after he'd sworn to himself that he wouldn't.

He trusted Lars and Nikki to protect her. Of course, he'd trusted Cole, too.

"I am sorry I took her out of the condo," Cole said. He must have mistaken Manny being quiet earlier for being angry with him.

He wasn't entirely wrong. "Why did you?" Manny asked.

"Can you say no to her?" Cole asked.

Manny cursed at himself more than Cole.

"Yeah, I didn't think so," his friend said.

"I wish I would have said no to Cooper," Manny said. "This is a wild-goose chase." He hadn't wanted to go himself and he certainly hadn't needed anyone along for his protection. But Teddie had been so worried about his going alone that Cooper had ordered Cole to accompany him.

The guy probably should have gone to the ER instead. But he'd seemed fine when Manny had flown them to New York. Actually, since he had seemed fine, he probably really needed to get his head checked out. Cole usually hated riding with anyone else. They always rock-paper-scissored over piloting the plane.

Cole held up a folder he'd taken from a drawer of the desk in front of the windows. Just like the one at the cabin, this desk was piled high with textbooks. Teddie was determined to get the education she wanted. From the looks of the penthouse, she already had everything else.

"It's not a wild-goose chase," Cole said. "The file was right where she said it would be."

Of course it was. He took it from Cole's hand and flipped through the letters in the folder. Several were of a couple, her image cut out and pasted to stand beside an insipid-looking young man. The images weren't damaged, though. And there were no threats with them, just declarations of admiration. Manny shook his head. "This is a wild-goose chase because I don't think her stalker ever sent her a *fan* letter."

Cole took the folder back and flipped through the pages himself. "Is there one from you in here? Is that why you didn't want to get these?"

Manny snorted. Even though he'd had her poster, he would have never considered writing her a letter. To him she'd never been real. And even now…

Even after making love with her…

He glanced around the penthouse and out the windows, where the lights of the city glittered like brightly colored stars. She wasn't real. This wasn't a life he could ever imagine.

"I'm not a letter writer," he said. "Just ask my mom." He'd never had much time to write letters. He hadn't had time for this trip, either. "The reason I didn't want to make this flight is because I'm already pretty damn certain who her stalker is."

"Who?" Cole asked.

"That photographer."

"And she said it wasn't," Cole reminded him. "She

dated the guy, so I'm pretty sure she would have recognized him."

"That's why he wears the masks," Manny said. "Hell, he could even be wearing colored contacts, so she doesn't recognize his eyes."

Cole narrowed his blue eyes and studied Manny. "That's true." But he sounded as if he still had his doubts.

"What?" Manny asked.

"It's almost like you want it to be him," Cole said. "Jealous?"

Manny snorted again. He had no right to jealousy. "Yeah, right."

"He is a good-looking guy," Cole said.

"I don't care what he looks like," Manny said. "I just care that someone has been terrorizing Teddie. And it needs to stop. We need to stop him."

"You care about her," Cole said.

"She's a client," Manny said as he headed for the door. "That's all she is."

Cole snorted now. "That's not all she is to *you*."

His friend knew him too well. It wasn't all she was. But it was all she could be. Seeing her penthouse—where and how she lived—reinforced the fact that they were too different. She could never be satisfied with a simple guy like him, a simple life like his.

No. She'd turned to him only for protection. And a distraction.

Unfortunately, she had distracted him, as well. But looking around her place, he knew this was where she belonged. He needed to help her get her life back with no threats from the stalker. And he needed to make certain that she was safe.

Just as she had convinced Cole to let her out of the condo, she might have convinced Lars and Nikki to do the same. If the stalker got to her before he returned…

He had to get back to River City. Now. But before he could open the door, the handle rattled, then began to turn. He grabbed for his gun just as it opened. Maybe the stalker had gotten fixated on him as well as Teddie. Or he knew what Manny had vowed—that the only way he would get to her was by taking out Manny first.

Seeing Manny draw his gun had Cole reaching for his, as well—even though he hadn't heard anyone at the door, hadn't seen the knob turn. But he saw the door open, saw the shock on the face of the man who stared into the barrels of two guns.

His face paled and he gasped. "What—who the hell…?"

Manny grabbed the man's neck and threw him against the wall next to the door. "You son of a bitch."

It wasn't the photographer Manny had thought it was. But this man's picture had been pinned to Nikki's wall of suspects, as well.

Manny had been right. The fan letters were a dead-end lead. But retrieving them might have helped them catch her stalker, if that was who this man was.

They needed to interrogate him. But Cole wasn't certain Manny would give the man the chance to speak. He'd tightened his hand around the guy's neck, like the stalker had choked Teddie in the hospital.

And Cole had a horrible feeling he might have to turn his gun on his friend—to stop him from becoming a killer.

Chapter 20

We got him. That was the text Cole had sent Nikki
from New York. At least, Cole thought they had him,
Nikki had informed Teddie. But Manny hadn't been
as convinced, so he hadn't called the police. Instead
they'd brought her stalker back to River City.

To the Payne Protection Agency.

And for some reason, maybe just to get close to Teddie again, the stalker had come along willingly.

Teddie stood outside the conference room, bracing
herself to confront the man who had made her life a
living hell the past few months. Nobody had told her
who it was, but apparently it was someone she knew.

"Are you ready?" Nikki asked.

The female bodyguard hadn't left her side since
she'd taken over protection duty from Manny. But even
with her sticking so close, Teddie hadn't felt safe. It

wasn't because Nikki was so petite. Despite her size, the female bodyguard was fierce. She was also armed. And her fiancé—the blond hulk—had always been close by, as well.

The reason Teddie hadn't felt safe was that Manny had been gone. It wasn't just her own safety about which she'd been concerned, though. She'd been more worried about Manny. And even though Cooper had sent another bodyguard along with him for his protection, it had been Cole, who was hurt. So he might not have been much help if the stalker had tried for Manny again.

And he must have. How else had they caught him?

"You don't have to do this," Nikki said when Teddie hesitated. "You don't have to face him."

"You said he wants to talk to me."

"Of course he does," Nikki said. "The whole point of stalking you is to get close to you."

He hadn't just wanted to get close to her, though. He'd wanted to hurt her. Kill her...

How could someone hate her that much?

She shuddered but nodded. "I want to talk to him."

She wanted to know why. What had she done?

Nikki opened the door to the conference room and held it for Teddie. The first person her gaze settled on wasn't the stalker but Manny. He was the one she wanted most to see, to make certain he was all right.

She'd been worried about him, worried that he might get hurt because of her. She breathed a sigh of relief that he looked fine, especially with his dark hair and dark eyes and strong jaw. He was so damn handsome.

Her pulse quickened, and she released a shaky breath. Then he stepped aside, and she saw the man sitting at the conference table. Was this who they thought her stalker was?

She shook her head. "No. This is a mistake."

Ed Bowers jerked his head up and down in a series of quick nods. "That's what I told them," he said. "This is all a mistake. But they wouldn't listen to me. That's why I agreed to come here, so I could explain it to you."

She glanced at Manny now. "You didn't hurt him, did you?"

Her old manager wasn't as big and strong and young as he and Cole were.

"If it's a mistake, what the hell was he doing letting himself into your penthouse?" It was Cole who asked the question while Manny stayed curiously silent.

She glanced at Ed now. "How—why…?" It wasn't possible, was it? A man who had been almost like a father to her couldn't have betrayed her, could he?

Not that Teddie had any idea what a father was supposed to be like. She'd never met hers.

"I still have the extra set you gave me when you bought the penthouse," Ed explained. "I'd forgotten I had them until I saw the news. Then I remembered the keys and those creepy fan letters you used to get. I intended to get them and bring them to the police department."

"You should have brought him to the police department," Cooper said from the end of the conference table.

She glanced at her bodyguard. That was all he was now. There was nothing of her lover on his handsome face, no memory of the intimacy they'd shared. He was all business.

"I wanted to," Cole said defensively. "But Manny wanted to bring him here instead."

"I didn't bring him to the police department because he's not the guy," Manny explained to his boss.

"But he has keys to her penthouse like the stalker had keys to the cabin," Cole pointed out. "And he has motive." He gestured at the board now.

Teddie shook her head. "I gave Ed those keys when I first bought the place. I didn't give him keys to the cabin. And he has no motive to hurt me."

Ed looked at her now. "You know I would never hurt you."

And she believed him. That was why he had told her she needed to find another agent. He'd thought he was hurting her career because he couldn't keep up with all the jobs designers had wanted to book her for.

She settled onto the chair across from him, reached over the table and squeezed his hand. "I know."

"That's why—once I saw the news and found out you have a stalker—I wanted to get those old fan letters," Ed said. "I wanted to see if they would help the police figure out who's trying to hurt you."

"Did you get the letters?" Nikki asked.

Cole handed over a folder to the female bodyguard. "There are some weird ones in there. But that doesn't mean he couldn't have sent them." It was clear he still suspected Ed.

Teddie didn't. She couldn't.

"It'll be simple enough to check his alibi for the most recent attempts," Manny said.

Ed squeezed her hand and stared at her across the table. "I'm so sorry to hear about what you've been going through. I had no idea when you dropped out of the public eye that that was why."

She should have stayed in touch with Ed. But she'd

felt so bad about no longer working with him that she hadn't wanted to burden him with her problems. Or endanger him. It looked like she had anyway, since he looked a little roughed up with his hair disheveled and his clothes rumpled.

But he asked her, "Are you okay, honey?"

She forced her lips to curve up at the corners. But that was the biggest smile she could manage.

So of course he wasn't fooled. "You were smart to hire the Payne Protection Agency," he said.

"It was Mama's idea," she said. If she hadn't listened to her mother, she probably would have been dead—at the least. At the worst…

She shuddered to think about what the stalker might have done to her. But she had only to look at those mutilated photographs to remember his intentions.

"Your mother is a very shrewd woman," Ed said. He had always had a soft spot for Mama. But her mother had never believed a man who worked with models could have been genuinely interested in her. In her mind she was still the trailer trash Teddie's father had called her.

"How is she?" Ed asked.

"Worried sick," Teddie admitted.

He glanced behind him—at Manny. "Me, too." He'd said she'd been smart to hire Payne Protection. So what about Manny could concern him?

Was he worried that she might fall for the man? Because she was worried that she already had.

Manny had insisted on being the one to bring Teddie back to the condo. Maybe all the talk of her mother had reminded him of his promise to the woman. Or maybe it was because he'd promised himself. Either way, he knew it was a mistake when the steel door closed behind them, locking them inside the safe house together.

Just the two of them…

"Thank you," she said.

"I'm just doing my job," he said, reminding her and himself that was all this was. A professional relationship. Not a real one. Seeing her penthouse had proved that to him.

"If you'd just been doing your job…" she began.

He wouldn't have slept with her. Was she going to bring that up?

But she continued, "You would have brought Ed to the police department like Cooper wanted. And if the press had gotten wind of that, it could have ruined his career."

"He's not the guy," Manny said. And it hadn't taken Nikki long to prove his alibi was legit. She'd hacked into a hotel's security feeds and proved he'd been at the charity ball just like he'd claimed. He wasn't the guy. The stalker was still out there. That was why it had been important to get Teddie back to the safe house.

But it didn't feel safe anymore, at least not to Manny. Being alone with her was dangerous as hell—for him.

"I know," Teddie said, "but the media doesn't care about facts. Just knowing he'd been brought in would have damaged his reputation."

"You care about him," Manny said.

"He's a good guy," she insisted. "He would never try to hurt me."

"No," Manny agreed. "He's scared of your mother, too."

Teddie laughed. "*You're* scared of my mother?"

"Terrified," he said.

"She would love that." She smiled a genuine smile that brightened her green eyes, not a fake smile like the one Manny had seen her force for her former manager. "She would love you."

He shook his head. "I told you—mothers don't like me. Sometimes not even my own." He'd reminded her too much of his father. That was why he'd been so careful to act nothing like him.

Teddie's smile slipped away. "That's terrible."

He shrugged. "I understand. The men in my family don't exactly inspire trust."

"My mother trusts you," Teddie said. "I spoke with her earlier tonight. She believes you'll keep me safe."

Manny felt a pressure on his chest, panic that he might fail not just her mother but her. "I shouldn't have made her any promises."

"You won't keep me safe?" Teddie asked. And the smile was back, playing around her full lips as she teased him.

That pressure increased. "I'll do my best." And hopefully this time his best would be good enough.

She stared up at him, her green eyes darkening with desire. His heart pounded with it. But he couldn't give in to temptation again, not when he knew that he would never be good enough for her.

He expelled a ragged breath and told her, "You have a real fancy place in New York."

"I do," she agreed. "I don't know why I bought it."

So she wasn't just renting the penthouse. Not that he knew anyone who would have even been able to afford the rent. Except for Cole. Cole probably could.

"Why don't you know?" he asked, wondering about her. Which woman was real? The supermodel living in the New York City penthouse? Or the student hiding out at a secluded, rustic cabin?

"I didn't need the penthouse," she said. "I think I only bought it to prove to myself how far I came from where I started."

"What do you mean?" he asked.

She sighed. "I already told you that my mom was just a kid when she had me. Her parents had ditched her for drugs, so she was living in a trailer with her grandmother."

Manny had even more respect for her mother now.

"Mama wanted out of the trailer badly since that was why my dad had dumped her—because she was just trailer trash. So when Nana passed away," she continued, "she used the leftover life insurance to buy a little house for us. But we could barely make ends meet. It was tough for Mama to get a good-paying job since she'd dropped out of school to have me. So to help her out, I started babysitting when I was eleven."

"Just a kid yourself."

She nodded, then shuddered. "Not all the dads saw me that way, though. I developed early."

Anger surged through Manny. "Did someone hurt you?" He would go back and kill him, whoever he was.

She shook her head. "No. But one creepy dad tried to convince me to let him take pictures of me."

Yeah, he wanted to kill the guy. "Is he still alive?" Maybe her stalker went way back in her life.

She shook her head again. "No. He passed away years ago. He said he wanted to send the pictures to some modeling competition for me."

"You didn't let him take the pictures, did you?" he asked, horrified for her.

"No. I told Mama, and she took care of him."

No wonder the guy wasn't alive anymore. "I do like your mom," he mused.

"But I told Mama to take the pictures," she said. "We had to save up for a good camera first. And she wouldn't do it until I was older—fifteen. Those were the photos we entered in that suntan-lotion contest."

Photos she probably wouldn't have taken if not for the creepy dad. Manny still wanted to hurt him, though, for objectifying a child.

"You won that contest," he remembered from her telling him and from what he'd already known about her.

"Yes," she said. "Probably because Ed was one of the judges. He offered me representation." She sighed. "I shouldn't have left his agency."

Manny hoped Nikki had double-checked that security footage to make sure it wasn't tampered with. The guy might have had a legit gripe with Teddie. But then he remembered Ed Bowers's very genuine concern.

"The only thing your old manager seems upset about is your being in danger," Manny said. He believed the guy, believed that he had only wanted to help when he'd let himself into her penthouse.

"He's not the only one," Teddie said. "I want this to be over. That's why I think we should let the stalker get me again."

"What!" Manny exclaimed.

"Using Nikki as a decoy to try to flush him out didn't work," she reminded him. "An impostor won't fool him. But we know that if I'm out again—on my own—he will grab me."

"That's why you're not leaving here again," Manny said. "You're staying where it's safe."

"But I would be safe out there," she said, "if all of you were close. It's probably the only way we'll be able to catch him."

He shook his head. "No. We'll figure out who he is without putting your life at risk."

"What kind of life am I living?" she asked. "When I'm always afraid? When I can't go anywhere, can't do anything? I don't want to live like this."

He could understand her frustration. "Just give us a little while longer," he said. "Nikki's looking into all those old letters."

She shook her head. "None of those were sent by the stalker. She's wasting her time."

Manny was afraid that she was probably right. But there had to be some other way to catch the stalker than putting her at risk. He couldn't take the chance of losing her.

When they caught the stalker, he would. She would go back to her old life and he would move on to the next assignment. They had no future together. But he wanted to make sure she would have a future.

"You hired us to protect you," he reminded her. "Let us do our job."

"Is that all I am to you?" she asked.

This question was far more dangerous—to him—than her asking to flush out the stalker. Because he wasn't sure he could be truthful with her or with himself.

Nikki sucked in a breath as the police record scrolled across her screen. She glanced down at the spliced photo of Teddie and the man Nikki had run through the face recognition program she had.

His face had gotten a hit on a mug shot. He'd been booked for assault and battery, for stalking…

This had to be the guy. But this letter wasn't like the others. He didn't threaten her harm. Instead he declared his love and adoration and intention to one day meet and marry her. It was creepy. But it wasn't as creepy as the others.

Had he escalated?

Obviously he was capable of violence or he wouldn't have a police record.

"Did you find her guy?" Cooper asked as he peered at the monitor over Nikki's shoulder.

She shrugged. "I don't know if it's the same stalker we've been dealing with or another one."

"You think she might have two?"

"It's possible she could have two stalkers," Nikki said. Teddie Plummer was in serious peril.

Chapter 21

Manny hadn't answered her question. He just stared at her. "I'm sorry," she said. "I didn't mean to put you on the spot like that. Of course I'm just an assignment to you. I know that."

He pressed a finger across her lips and murmured, "And people say I talk too much…"

"You?" His finger brushed her lips as she spoke the single word. And she shivered at the sensation.

Manny's eyes dilated until the brown turned black with desire. "I guess I don't with you."

They did things other than talk when they were alone together. They kissed. They made love.

She wanted to do that now. But first she needed to know that she meant something to him.

And finally he told her, "You're more—much more—than just an assignment to me."

"So you don't sleep with every client you protect?" she asked. She'd meant to sound as if she was just teasing him, but her real fear had crept into her voice.

He shook his head. "No. Lars and Dane would have killed me if we did. Our first job was rescuing Lars's sister. Our second was keeping her safe."

She smiled. "I understand why Lars would kill you if you slept with his sister. But why Dane?"

"Because he'd fallen for Lars's sister," Manny explained. "And yes, Lars did nearly kill Dane."

"But he and Nikki..." She was his boss's sister. And she suspected Cooper Payne was more than just a boss to these men. He was a friend, as well.

Manny chuckled. "Yeah, Lars is a big old hypocrite."

She laughed, too, even as she felt a pang of jealousy at his friendships. She wished she had friends like his, ones she could trust.

"You're lucky," she said wistfully, "to have them."

"Yeah, I am," he agreed. "But don't ever tell them I admitted that to you."

His friendships were unlike anything she knew, not just because he could trust the other men, but also because of how they treated each other. Teddie, growing up with just her mom, had no idea about male relationships—with each other or with her.

Maybe that was why she'd never gotten serious with anyone before. She'd had no idea how romance functioned. She and work had been her mother's entire focus. Mama had rarely dated, and when she had, she hadn't brought many of the men home to meet Teddie.

And Teddie hadn't brought any home to meet Mama.

She hadn't let herself trust or care about anyone enough to keep them around. Until now…

But Manny wasn't someone she should trust to stick around, either. Once this assignment was complete, he would move on to the next one, which would probably be just as dangerous as this one.

But it seemed to be what he enjoyed doing, he and his friends. Risking their lives for others.

"I don't understand you," she admitted.

Manny sighed. "Since meeting you, I don't understand myself." He leaned down so his forehead pressed against hers. And he stared into her eyes. "I don't do this."

"This?" she asked, her heart pounding frantically at the look in his eyes. The desire and something else, something deeper…

Or was it only her wishful thinking that there was more? Was it just a reflection of what she was feeling for him?

"I don't get distracted," he said.

"I'm a distraction?"

"Just like you're more than an assignment, you're more than a distraction," he said. "You're…"

She waited but he said nothing more. So she prodded, "What? What am I?"

"Everything," he murmured. Then he kissed her—deeply, passionately. His tongue slid between her lips and stroked over hers.

She reached up and clutched the nape of his neck, holding his head down to hers as she kissed him back. His hair tickled her fingers, making them tingle.

He touched her, too, and she tingled everywhere. He

moved his hands from her waist down to her thighs.
Then he cupped her butt in his palms and lifted her.

She wrapped her legs around his waist and rocked
her hips against the erection straining against the fly
of his jeans. Heat flooded her. Her intensity frightened
her because she didn't just want him. She *needed* him.

She needed him not just to make love to her but also
to love her. Because she loved him.

The realization both terrified and thrilled her. She
had fallen in love with her bodyguard. And it was both
scary to be this open and exhilarating to finally feel
this much...

Love.

He carried her to the bedroom. He must have been
feeling the same intensity of desire that she was because he undressed her quickly, pulling off her sweater
and pushing down her pants until she stood naked before him. But it wasn't just her body that was bared to
him; her heart and soul were, too.

She had never been so vulnerable. How could she
have fallen so hard, so fast? But she hadn't been able
to stop herself, hadn't been able to hold back as she
always had. Because this was Manny.

He was special.

As he took off his holster, she took off the rest of his
clothes, unclasping his belt and unbuttoning his jeans.
When she pulled down the tab of his zipper, his erection burst free, pushing against his boxers. She stroked
her hand over him, and he groaned.

"Teddie..." He kissed her again.

Then she was the one groaning as he moved his
mouth down to her breasts. He teased her nipples with
his lips and his tongue before he moved lower yet,

dropping to his knees in front of her. And he made love to her with his mouth.

She cried out as she came. Her knees gave out and she dropped down to the bed. After sheathing himself in latex, he followed her down, moving between her legs. He stroked in and out of her until the tension built inside her again. She dug her nails lightly in his shoulders before moving them down his rippling back to the tight muscles of his butt.

He was so damn perfect. So sexy…

He moved his hand between their bodies and stroked his finger over the most sensitive part of her. And she came again, crying out his name. She might have said more, might have declared her love.

But he kissed her deeply. Then he groaned in her mouth as his body tensed and he came, too. His big body shuddered against hers.

He left her, but only for a few seconds, before he came back and pulled her into his arms. He held her closely, protectively.

She settled her head onto his shoulder and snuggled against him. While she loved this, while she loved him, she wanted her life back. She didn't want him to be with her because he was paid to be with her or because he'd promised her mother he'd protect her from the stalker.

She wanted the stalker out of her life. Forever.

She knew what she had to do. But she also knew that Manny wasn't going to like it. She might get her life back, but she wasn't sure he would be part of it any longer.

Now Manny knew how Dane had felt when they'd all agreed to let Emilia risk her life to save his. They'd had good intentions then to protect Emilia and rescue Dane. But Dane hadn't needed rescuing.

Teddie did, though. She needed rescuing from her own crazy scheme.

"This isn't going to work," he protested. But nobody listened to him.

Nikki and Teddie talked about self-defense, with Nikki showing her some moves at the end of the conference room. Dane and Lars talked about being invisible, so that the stalker wouldn't see them protecting Teddie and would attempt to grab her.

In the past Dane had been good at being invisible, but the stalker had already seen him—and nearly killed him—in those woods around the burned-down cabin.

They weren't going back to the UP, though. Or staying in River City. They were going to New York. No. Only Teddie was. Or at least that was how it would appear.

He shook his head. "This is crazy!"

Cooper and Cole glanced up from their conversation. And Cooper uttered a sigh of frustration. "We have no choice," he reminded Manny. His impatience wasn't with Manny or any member of his team. It was with their client, who refused to let them protect her how they saw fit. "She'll fire us if we don't agree."

Manny couldn't believe that she had made such a threat. He hadn't thought she was a prima donna, that she would do anything to get her way. Even risk her life.

Because if she fired them, the stalker would get her for certain, and there would be nobody to rescue her. Manny wouldn't have quit, though, no matter what she'd said. She would have had to take out a restraining order to stop him from protecting her.

And she still might need to.

"I have already fired you all," Teddie said, pointing toward the television screen on the wall of the conference room. Breaking news reported that supermodel Teddie Plummer didn't believe her life was really in danger, and that she'd fired the Payne Protection Agency. She'd called Bernard Setters with the story when Manny had fallen asleep.

So she had already set everything in motion. The stalker and any other kook who'd had an unnatural fascination with her would now think she had no protection.

"What you've done is put your life in even more danger than you already were in," he said. And he was furious with her for doing that. "Why?"

"I want my life back," she said.

He had been angry and afraid before. Now he was hurt. While he had admitted that she meant everything to him, he obviously meant nothing to her. Just like he had suspected, she wanted her old life back—the penthouse, the publicity, the money and fame.

Despite the size of her place in New York, there was no room in it for him—or in the lifestyle she wanted back so desperately that she was willing to risk her life for it.

He laughed as he watched the breaking news report. It was bogus. Another trick.

How stupid did she and her precious Payne Protection Agency think he was?

He knew her too well to fall for this trick. He knew

how smart she was and, more important, he knew how scared she was. Satisfaction filled him as he remembered her screams when he'd pulled her out of the SUV and into the van. She'd been terrified.

Too terrified and too smart to go out in public with no protection. He had also gotten to know her bodyguard. That guy wasn't smart, or he wouldn't have taken a job like his in which he risked his life for other people.

But Teddie wasn't just a client to him. There was no way Jordan Mannes would quit even if she fired him because the guy was every bit as obsessed with her as he was.

He laughed again as he realized how he could double-cross them both. He would teach that bodyguard for trying to take what was his.

And he would teach Teddie, once and for all, that she belonged to him. And only him.

Chapter 22

When Teddie had first come to New York, she'd been a small-town girl awed and impressed with the big city. Despite all the years she had lived there now, she was still that small-town girl. But she was no longer awed and impressed.

She would always visit it—for the theater and museums and music—but she never wanted to live here again. She didn't want to model anymore, either. But she took a few gigs just to draw out her stalker. Teddie Plummer returning from her early retirement was big news.

Since her return two weeks ago, nobody had tried to grab her yet. What had happened to her stalker?

Had he finally given up?

She didn't think so, because as she took her early-morning run, she could feel someone watching her.

And she didn't think it was just the Payne Protection bodyguards who hid in the park. It was someone else.

Her lungs burned from the cold, and her breaths as she panted were white puffs in the air. But it wasn't just the temperature that was chilling her blood. It was the set of eyes she could feel watching her.

Instead of being scared, though, she felt almost relieved. Finally he would try for her. Finally this would all be over, and she could live her life how she wanted and where she wanted.

But not with whom she wanted.

Manny was angry with her, so angry for forcing him and the Payne Protection Agency to go along with her plan. She doubted that he would forgive her.

Or trust her…

And she wasn't certain she blamed him. She had acted rashly. But she'd been desperate—desperate to end the danger. She hadn't realized how dangerous it might get.

She heard footsteps pounding the asphalt path behind her. It could have been another runner. There had been a few other ones who'd passed her despite the early hour and the low temperatures. But she didn't believe that was the case this time.

He was coming up on her too fast, too purposefully.

And then, before any of her bodyguards could step from their hiding places, he had her. He shoved her to the ground.

Her breath whooshed from her burning lungs as she hit the asphalt trail. Like when she'd jumped from the van, the pavement skinned her flesh, her elbow and her leg this time. And she cried out in pain and surprise.

Manny had warned her that her plan was too dangerous. She should have listened to him. But she could hear nothing now but the labored sounds of her own breathing. And his...

His hand fisted in her hair, pulling her up. Remembering the moves that Nikki had taught her, Teddie struck out with her elbow, sending it back into the man's chest. Then she turned and reached out for his eyes, clawing at them through the mask he wore.

"You bitch!" he yelled at her. And he raised his fist to strike her.

She closed her eyes and flinched. But the fist never connected. And the hand dropped from her hair. She heard grunts now and the crunch of bones. When she opened her eyes, she saw Manny standing over her assailant. The man lay in the fetal position on the ground.

Other bodyguards rushed from the shadows. Manny must have beaten them all to her.

Nikki helped her up from the ground and anxiously asked, "Are you okay?"

She nodded. When she could speak, she would thank Nikki for teaching her better moves than she'd learned in that self-defense class she'd taken. But even with her new knowledge, she wouldn't have been able to save herself from her stalker. She'd needed Manny.

But then, she needed Manny for more than protection.

"Do you recognize him?" Cooper asked the question.

And finally she turned toward the guy. Manny must have pulled off his mask. Or maybe she had when she'd clawed at his face. He had scratches on his pale skin. His face was narrow, his cheekbones and chin pointy, like some kind of animal. He looked like one now, the kind that had been caged and was desperate to escape. He wriggled and twisted in Manny's tight grasp.

She shook her head. "No. I don't know him."

"He's the guy," Nikki said. "The one who sent you those earlier letters. Herman Miner. He has a police record."

He was the fan who'd cut out the pictures of her and himself. He was just a fan. Not someone she had known and trusted.

She released her breath in a shuddery sigh of relief. It was over. It was finally over.

Her relief turned to a hard knot of regret as she focused on Manny's face. He wasn't relieved. He was still angry, his jaw rigid and lips drawn in a tight line.

It was over—with him.

It wasn't over.

"He's not the guy," Manny insisted even as a police officer loaded the man into the back of a squad car.

Cooper sighed as if he'd already grown tired of arguing with Manny. "He attacked her."

"He sent those letters," Nikki added.

"The first ones," Manny agreed. "You can't prove he sent those other ones."

"He attacked her." Nikki repeated what her brother had said. "He's already on probation for assault. So he'll go back to prison for a long time. He won't be able to hurt her anymore."

Manny would have been relieved had he actually believed this was the guy. But it wasn't. "Even you thought she could have two stalkers," he reminded Nikki.

"Do you want her to have two stalkers?" Nikki asked, and a slightly mocking smile curved her lips.

"Of course not."

But he didn't think he had been wrong about the photographer. Manny had been close enough to the stalker—more than once—to recognize the guy's build. And the photographer looked more the size of the guy who had taken out Dane and Cole than the thinner guy sitting in the back of the police car.

Nikki leaned close and whispered to him, "You don't need an excuse to stay close to her."

But he did. Otherwise he would be going back to River City, and Teddie would be staying here—in New York. This was what she'd wanted. She'd told him that already. She wanted her life back.

Maybe Nikki was right, and he was just looking for excuses to hang on to her. He walked over to Teddie sitting in the back of an ambulance. A paramedic cleaned the scrape on her leg and elbow.

The guy had hurt her. No matter if he was the real stalker or not, he deserved to go back to prison for attacking another woman.

"Are you all right?" he asked her.

She flashed him a smile, the same one that had graced so many magazine covers. "Yes. It's over."

Her happiness had pain gripping his heart. Sure, she should be thrilled that the stalker was caught. If he was really her stalker...

But was she also thrilled she no longer had any reason to have a bodyguard? Was she happy that she no longer needed him?

"You really think that's him?" he asked her. "The guy from the hospital?"

She glanced toward the back of the police car and furrowed her brow. "Of course it's him. It has to be."

But it didn't have to be. Just because the guy had tried to grab her in the park didn't mean he was also the one who'd followed her to the UP and to River City.

"Does it?" he asked. "He doesn't seem as big as the guy I fought with outside the cabin during the fire."

She glanced from him to the police car again. "How can you tell? It was so dark and smoky then."

"I just don't think he's the guy," he admitted.

And her smile slipped away. "You are determined to think that it's someone I know—like Ed or Anthony. What—do you want me to be as bad a judge of character as your dad and brother are?"

He flinched.

And she gasped. "I'm sorry."

"You admitted yourself you haven't always chosen the best friends," he reminded her. "I think it has to be someone you know or he wouldn't have worn a mask."

"This guy wore a mask," she said. "And I don't know him. I've never met him before. I've never seen him except in that picture he sent me."

Manny reminded her, "He sent that a long time ago and never tried to grab you before now."

"That you know of," she said. "What's wrong—why don't you want me to be safe?"

"It's because I want you to be safe that we need to make sure we've really got the guy," he persisted. The real stalker would love it if they let down their guard. Then he would have no problem grabbing her and keeping her.

Clearly exasperated with him, she sighed. "Okay, check him out."

"Good." The tight pressure in Manny's chest eased, but just slightly. "We'll stay with you until we know for sure that we got the right guy."

"Manny, I hope—"

"Miss Plummer," someone yelled out. And cameras flashed. "Teddie!" The paparazzi had found her. Bernard Setters and a few other reporters swarmed the ambulance. Manny stepped between her and the cameras, trying to protect her.

But he had a feeling no matter what anyone else believed, she needed protecting from more than the press yet. The stalker—the real stalker—was still out there, waiting to strike.

Would Manny be able to save her again—like he had this time? Or was his luck running out?

Cooper settled into one of the back seats of Cole's plane for the flight to River City. Dane sat in the front next to Cole, just about gripping whatever he could in the cockpit even though the plane hadn't been cleared to take off yet. Dane didn't like to fly. But he was as eager to get home as Cooper was.

They had their guy. They no longer needed to stay in New York.

But Manny had refused to leave yet.

He probably had an ulterior motive for staying. Teddie...

But Nikki and Lars had stayed behind, as well. Nikki had promised Manny she would sift back through the past couple of weeks of the stalker's life and make certain he was their guy. Cooper suspected she and Lars just wanted a chance to enjoy the city.

He didn't blame them. Hell, he didn't blame Manny,

either, if he was just looking for an excuse to stick close to Teddie Plummer. But Cooper had this slight nagging sensation himself. Knowing who the best person was to talk to about that, he pulled out his cell and pushed his mother's contact.

"Hey, sweetheart," she greeted him. She sounded a bit breathless as if she'd rushed to the phone. Of course, his mother was always rushing around—planning other people's weddings. She had help now. Lars's sister worked for her. Mom also had a husband now, too.

Maybe that was why she sounded out of breath.

"Is this a bad time?" he asked.

"Of course not," she said. "I just got in the door from the chapel, and Woodrow isn't home yet from the police department." Her husband, a former FBI chief special agent, was the new chief of the River City PD.

He relaxed a little—as much as he could relax with the tight knot of apprehension in his stomach. "Okay. Glad I'm not interrupting anything."

Penny Payne-Lynch laughed. "If that's the case then you better talk fast, sweetheart. My husband will be home soon."

She sounded so happy, happier than he ever remembered his mother sounding. Usually her happiness would have warmed his heart and eased his tension.

But not now.

"That's fine," he said. "I shouldn't have bothered you anyway."

"Nonsense," she said. "What's up?"

"I don't know," he admitted. "I thought we wrapped up our current assignment, but I'm feeling a little uneasy."

Dane and Cole glanced back at him. And now they looked like he felt.

"Uneasy?" his mother asked.

He sighed and admitted, "I got one of your weird feelings."

"That something bad's going to happen?"

He couldn't ignore the knots tightening his stomach muscles. "Yes."

"But you said you wrapped up the assignment."

"I think we did," he said. "I think we got the guy. But Manny doesn't."

Dane snorted. "He wants an excuse to stick close to Teddie Plummer."

That was what Nikki thought, too. But Cooper's gut was telling him something else, that maybe Manny could be right.

"Listen to your instincts," his mother advised. "You've got good ones."

Yes, he did—because he had hers. "Thanks, Mom."

"So, are we leaving or not?" Cole asked when Cooper clicked off his cell. "I'm cleared for takeoff."

Cooper hesitated. He really wanted to get home to his beautiful bride, to his kids. He could see Dane wanted to get back to Emilia and Blue, as well.

But what if Manny was right…?

Before Cooper could answer Cole, his cell rang, and he recognized Teddie Plummer's number. "Here's the client now."

He would have rather heard from Nikki and gotten confirmation that they had the right guy. But he clicked the connect button. "Hello?"

"You're fired!" Teddie yelled, her voice cracking with emotion.

"Fired?" The case was wrapping up anyway—hopefully. But she had agreed to let them check out the stalker before they considered the assignment ended. At least, that was what Manny had claimed. "I don't understand."

"Turn on the news, then," she said, and now her voice cracked with tears. "I can't believe he betrayed me like this."

"Who? What are you talking about?" he asked.

"No." She sucked in a breath. "I should have expected it. I've learned I can't trust anyone."

"Who?" he asked again.

"Manny," she replied. "I'm firing Payne Protection. You should fire him." Before he could get a more detailed explanation from her, she hung up.

He stared at the cell phone screen for a long moment. Confused. "Why the hell would she want me to fire Manny?" he wondered aloud.

Dane reached between the seats and showed Cooper the screen on his cell. A news report played out with pictures of Teddie Plummer and her bodyguard, who had told the press all about their sordid affair.

"Manny must have run his mouth," Dane said, shaking his head.

Cole glanced over at Dane's screen and shook his head. "No. He wouldn't have done that."

"Manny likes to talk," Dane said.

Cooper continued to watch the report. "He knows when not to talk, though."

Manny had held his silence regarding the secret missions they'd carried out during their years in the Corps. And he had never talked to the press regarding the other assignments the Payne Protection Agency had had.

"He wouldn't have done it," Cole insisted.

"Then how the hell did the media get ahold of that story?" Dane asked. "And the photos?"

Cooper wondered, too, especially about the photos. Manny certainly wouldn't have taken those. But a woman who modeled swimsuits and lingerie would have no qualms about the skin she'd bared. Of course, the ones the media showed had been blurred.

"Was it all just a stunt?" he asked. "Did she contact the press herself?"

Dane touched the back of his head. "She didn't sneak up and hit me, though."

"No," Cooper agreed. "She must have hired someone to act like he was stalking her."

Cole cursed. "Damn it. Poor Manny. I think he was actually falling for her."

He would be devastated to learn she'd used him. Hell, she'd used the entire Payne Protection Agency. But Manny was the one who was going to be hurt the most.

"So, do we take off?" Cole asked.

"Yes," Cooper said. The only danger Manny was in was of having his heart broken. But that might be the greatest danger of all.

Chapter 23

Her stomach churning with dread, Teddie stared at the television screen. How could he have done this to her?

It could have only been Manny. Only he knew that they'd crossed the line—unless he'd told his friends. But then there were the photos, too.

He must have somehow taken them with his phone. But how? And when? How had she not noticed if he'd set it up to snap photos of them? Of course, she had been distracted—enthralled—with him.

It had to be him. No one else could have taken those photos. It wasn't like someone could have used a tele-photo lens, not through the blinds. They were all from inside the cabin.

And what he'd told the reporter…

About her trailer-trash mom, about her dad never wanting anything to do with her.

Only a few people knew the truth. And until now, until she'd told Manny, it had never made the news. More photos played across the screen, of him carrying her to the ambulance with the cabin burning in the background. Of him rescuing her in the park...

The news called him her hero. But a hero wouldn't have betrayed her like he had.

How could he have done it? Why?

For money. She knew he must not make much. She'd seen his apartment. But she hadn't thought he cared about money.

God, she'd been so naive. Everyone cared about money, more than they cared about people.

The door rattled as the knob turned. She'd given him a key to the penthouse. She'd trusted him with that. She'd trusted him with so much.

Her hand shaking, she wiped the tears she hadn't even realized she'd been crying from her cheeks. And she turned to face that door.

He smiled as he stepped inside, a bag of takeout dangling from his fingers along with her keys. His other hand was sliding his gun back into his holster.

She swallowed hard. But it wasn't fear she felt. It was fury. "You don't need the gun," she told him.

His brow furrowed. "What—did Nikki prove he's your guy?"

She'd wanted Manny to be her guy, to be the person on whom she could count the most. The one she could trust. But he'd failed her.

She shook her head. "I haven't heard from Nikki yet." But she didn't need to. She doubted there was anyone else after her.

"Then I need this," Manny said. "You could still be in danger."

"Not anymore." She had been hurt worse than she'd ever been hurt. Her heart was broken—shattered—by his betrayal.

He narrowed his dark eyes and studied her expression. "What's wrong?" he asked. As he stepped closer, he reached up to touch her face.

But she stepped back. "Don't touch me! Don't ever touch me again!"

"What's going on?" he asked. Then he finally saw it, the TV playing behind her. And he gasped. "How the hell— Where did those photos come from?"

"You tell me," she said. "When did you take them?"

He shook his head. "I—I didn't."

"You must have—with your phone."

"What phone? My first one was dead." He moved around her to the screen and touched one of the photos that had to have been taken before the other bodyguard had arrived in the UP.

She had let him use hers to call Cooper. Manny must have taken one then with her phone and sent it to himself. "How could you?" she asked.

"How could I what?" he repeated.

She gripped the remote and turned up the volume so the reporter's words echoed off the walls, words he claimed Manny had told him. He had no reason to lie about his source. The only person with a reason to lie was Manny.

He shook his head and cursed, "That son of a bitch."

"You didn't think he would tell who gave him the story," she mused. "How much did he pay you? How much did you get…?" To break her heart?

He turned toward her now, and his eyes were wide with shock and what must have been feigned innocence. How could he keep lying to her? "You think I would do this?" he asked. "You think I would talk to reporters, that I would tell anyone the things you told me?"

If that was his attempt to convince her, he hadn't. It was weak, so weak that she laughed, albeit bitterly.

"I hadn't thought so," she admitted. "Or I wouldn't have been so open with you. I thought I could trust you. But I don't know why. You warned me from the beginning that you came from a family of criminals. Not that it's a crime to break someone's trust." But it should have been.

"It's not a crime to sell a story to the media, either," she continued. "As for taking the pictures without my knowledge, I can probably take you to court for that. But then, I might have to see you again. And I'd never want that."

It hurt too much. When she had first seen the news, she'd felt like her heart had been ripped out. Now she knew that Manny held it in his big hands, crushing it. Her chest ached and felt so hollow. She felt so empty.

"*I* am not a criminal," he said, his voice full of anger and outrage.

She pointed at the TV again. "It wasn't exactly like robbing a bank. But it was close." She was the bank. And she'd never seen him coming.

He shook his head. And he actually had the gall to look disgusted.

"Get the hell out!" she shouted at him. "I already talked to Cooper. I already fired Payne Protection. Now I'm firing you."

He shook his head again. "You can't—"

"I already have," she said. "Get the hell out!"

"Teddie, you could still be in danger. We don't know—"

She laughed and now it wasn't just bitter. It was nearing hysteria. "Stop it! Stop trying to scare me into letting you stay."

She wasn't afraid anymore. The thing she'd always feared the most—getting her heart broken like her mother's heart had been broken when Teddie's father had used and tossed her aside—had happened now. She had been used, her heart broken, but she was tossing him aside before he could toss her.

"I'm not trying to scare you," he said.

"You're trying to stay—"

He ran a shaking hand over his face. And then something must have snapped inside him because he shouted back at her, "I don't want to stay! I don't want to be in the same room with someone who could think I would sell them out for money."

She flinched. But she refused to let him get to her. He'd already proved she couldn't trust him. "Then get out."

He started toward the door but turned back to ask, "You think I give a damn about money?"

"I don't know what you give a damn about," she admitted.

"You," he said. "I cared about you, about keeping you safe."

She had let herself believe that, had let herself hope that she was more than an assignment to him. Unfortunately, she had been. She'd been a payout.

He dropped the bag of food onto the table next to

the door and reached for the knob. His hand fisted over it, but he hesitated for a moment. Then he turned back and said, "Think about this. If I really wanted money, I wouldn't have sold a story about you. I would have tried to make you fall in love with me."

He hadn't had to try. She'd fallen willingly. Stupidly.

"I would have more money by sticking with you than by losing you," he pointed out. Had that been his plan all along?

"You never had me," she lied—because what he said hurt nearly as much as his betrayal.

"I know," he said. "You were just using me."

Because her pride hurt nearly as much as her aching heart, she lied some more. "Yes, I did just use you for sex. For protection. You never meant anything to me. You were just a bodyguard."

He flinched as if she'd slapped him. Just like she'd wanted—just like she'd tried—she had hurt him. But she didn't feel good about it. She didn't feel vindicated.

He said nothing more, just pulled open the door and walked out. As the door closed behind him, Teddie resisted the urge to call him back, to apologize. She knew she was wrong. But she wasn't sure what she was wrong about—hurting him or trusting him in the first place.

And now that she'd fired Payne Protection, she had to be careful. She had to protect herself. She wasn't worried about another stalker. She was worried that she might never be able to trust anyone again, not after Manny.

As a Marine, as a bodyguard even, Manny had been shot, stabbed and beaten. But no bullet or knife or fist had ever hurt him as badly as Teddie Plummer's words had. He stumbled out of the building foyer, feeling as if he was in shock. Cameras flashed in his face, blinding him like she'd blinded him with pepper spray that first time they'd met.

"Do you have any follow-up comments to the interview you gave Bernard Setters?" someone asked. "Any details about what supermodel Teddie Plummer enjoys most in the bedroom?"

Manny shoved his palm against the reporter's chest and flattened him against the wall of the building. "I did not give anyone an interview," he said.

"The pictures—"

"Nor did I give any pictures."

He turned back toward the crush of reporters and noticed someone slinking away from the group. And he headed after him. Bernard Setters tried to run. But he wasn't fast enough to escape Manny. He grabbed the back of his collar and drew him up short, his feet almost dangling above the sidewalk.

"Why the hell did you do that?" Manny demanded to know.

The guy gasped and sputtered and wriggled until his collar tore and he dropped to the concrete. "This— this is assault."

"And what you've done is slander," Manny said. At least he thought that was what it was. "And lies. I never gave you any photos. I never talked to *you* about Teddie."

Bernard shrugged. "I was given the photos and the story. Whoever gave it to me said they were you. Why would I doubt them?"

Why had Teddie doubted him?

He cursed. The damn stalker. He'd set up Manny. It was a brilliant plan, the perfect way to get Teddie to fire him. She denied it, but the stalker had to be someone who knew her well, who knew her even better than Manny did.

"I need everything you got," Manny told him.

"You didn't keep copies?" Bernard scoffed.

Manny reached for the guy again. But before his fist could connect, someone grabbed his arm and pulled him back. This person was big, even bigger than Manny. And strong, so strong that he held tightly to his fist and dragged him back.

"Settle down," Lars told him. "You're only making this worse."

The cameras hadn't stopped flashing, so Lars was right. Teddie would probably think Manny wanted this attention, wanted the limelight she'd claimed she'd wanted to escape.

Lars led him toward a rental car parked at the curb. Manny hopped into the passenger's seat, but when Lars slid behind the wheel, he caught his arm to stop him from turning the key in the ignition. "I don't think we should leave her alone."

He knew now—no matter what Nikki discovered—that there was another stalker out there.

"She fired Payne Protection," Lars said. "Cooper called from the plane. He wants to talk to you."

Manny groaned. "Does he think I sold out our client, too?"

Lars stared at him over the console, his pale blue eyes intense. "You are known for your big mouth."

Manny cursed. "Yeah, I talk too much—sometimes," he said. "But I would never sell any secrets."

Lars's head bobbed in a quick nod.

And Manny breathed a sigh of relief. "You know me." Thank God someone believed him. "Cooper must know…"

Or was he going to fire him? Was that why he wanted to talk to him?

If Manny lost his job, he would have to reenlist with the Corps. Being a bodyguard or a Marine was the only thing he knew.

"Cooper knows," Lars assured him. "He knows it wasn't you who talked."

"The stalker," Manny said. "That crazy fan isn't the real guy, not the one who hit Dane over the head and set the cabin on fire."

"No, it's not," Lars agreed. "Nikki had to dig a little but she found proof of that. She also talked to the guy. He claimed to get that ski mask in the mail along with a note telling him where he would be able to catch Teddie."

Manny swore a streak. "This guy is diabolical. He thinks of everything."

"He?" Lars asked.

"Of course," Manny said. "You think a woman would have been able to hit Dane that hard with a rock?" He grimaced as he thought of Lars's fiancée. Nikki hated being underestimated. And she was freakishly strong. "I'm sorry. I know Nikki can take out every one of us. But—"

"It wasn't Nikki," Lars said, his lips curving into a slight smile.

"I know that—"

"Cooper thinks Teddie set this whole thing up as a PR stunt."

Manny shook his head. "No…" He'd seen genuine fear on her face, in her voice. And when she'd pointed at that news story, she had looked hurt. Betrayed. Devastated.

"That's not possible," he said.

"Think about it," Lars said. "She probably hired someone to act like a stalker up at the cabin. And when she realized we weren't going to play along with her game forever, she set up a scapegoat in that *fan*."

"No…"

"She's the one who brought up those old letters," Lars reminded him. "She didn't want us thinking it was any of the suspects Nikki had developed. She didn't want anyone she knew getting in trouble for her stunt."

"So she'd send an innocent man to prison?"

Lars snorted. "You saw the guy's record. There's nothing innocent about him. And he didn't have to take that mask. He didn't have to show up at the park. While someone else had put the plan in motion, it was his choice to attack her."

Just like Manny's brother had chosen to rob that gas station and his father had chosen to hurt people he'd claimed to love.

But it had all begun with women, with falling for the wrong women…

Had Manny fallen for the wrong woman? Did he have the notorious Mannes poor judgment? "Why?"

Even though he asked himself the question, Lars answered, "For publicity. She's getting older. There are younger models popping up every day. This whole stalked-supermodel stunt puts her face on every television and subsequently every magazine and billboard."

She'd admitted she wanted her life back. Was this the one she'd wanted? The fame and fortune?

Was it all a ploy? Or was she really in danger?

Until she had fallen for Lars, Nikki had had some serious trust issues. After she had learned—in the proof of her illegitimate brother—that her father, the man she'd admired and idolized, had betrayed her mother, Nikki had lost all faith in men. In happily-ever-after.

Lars had restored her faith with his love. But sometimes she still struggled to trust. Like right now, she wasn't certain if Cooper was right and Teddie Plummer had used the Payne Protection Agency for publicity or if she and the stalker were for real.

But it didn't matter which was true. Either reason would have brought Nikki to the penthouse. She didn't care so much that Payne Protection had been used. She cared that Manny had. And she cared that Teddie might still be in danger if the stalker was real.

"I fired all of you," Teddie said as she opened the door. But she stepped back to let Nikki inside the penthouse.

Nikki nearly tripped over a bunch of bags sitting next to the door. "You're leaving?"

Teddie nodded and quickly closed the door behind her. "I need to get away."

"But isn't this what you wanted?" Nikki asked. And she pointed to the television set with Teddie's face running across it.

"What?" The supermodel shuddered. "I didn't want any of this. I can't believe Manny…"

"You shouldn't," Nikki said. "I can't believe that you actually do think he had anything to do with it."

"Bernard Setters—"

"—reported what he was told," Nikki said. "Printed what he was given. He doesn't know who really gave him those photos or that story."

Teddie shook her head. She was either unwilling or afraid to listen—to realize that she'd been wrong. "It could have only been Manny."

Nikki arched a brow. She had learned that from her mother. Sometimes it was all Penny Payne had needed to do to get people talking.

"What?" Teddie asked.

"You," Nikki said. "It could have been you."

Teddie's mouth dropped open in shock. "That—that's crazy."

"Other celebrities have pulled stunts like this, tried to extend their fifteen minutes of fame or resuscitate a dying career."

Teddie shook her head. "That's—"

"Insulting?" Nikki asked. But she felt no sympathy. Only anger for how this woman had treated her friend. "How the hell do you think Manny felt when you accused him of selling you out?"

"He did."

Nikki shook her head. "He did not."

"Even you told me he has a big mouth," Teddie reminded her.

"I said he talks a lot," Nikki said. "But he's always kept the secrets he's supposed to keep. And he would never betray someone he cares about."

Teddie blinked as if tears were threatening. From the dark circles and puffiness around her eyes, it looked as though she had been crying. She drew in a breath before replying, "Then I guess that proves he never cared about me."

"Bull." Nikki called her on it. "Even after how you've treated him, he asked me to come here."

"Of course he did," Teddie said. "To plead his case."

Nikki shook her head. "He doesn't give a damn what you think of him anymore." That was a lie. But she was still mad that this woman had hurt her friend. The fact that she was hurting, too, didn't change that. "He just wanted you to know that the guy in custody—the fan— he couldn't have been the guy up north."

Teddie shook her head. "What's with all of you?" she asked. "Are you so desperate for business that you don't want this assignment to end? Don't you have any other clients?"

Now Nikki was insulted. She lifted her chin. "What's with all of us?" she repeated. "We take our jobs seriously. We care about people and protecting them— whether they deserve our protection or not."

She turned toward the door. "Cooper's probably right about you. He has Mom's instincts, so I shouldn't have doubted him. You scammed us all. I hope the attention you wanted is worth what you lost."

But if Teddie really wanted attention, why was she leaving? Of course, Nikki didn't know where she was headed. She could have been off to Paris or LA. But the bags by the door looked more like what one would pack to go camping, not to go to a fashion show or movie premiere.

"What did I lose?" Teddie asked.

Nikki glanced back at her. "A great guy. Someone you can trust. You broke his heart."

Teddie shook her head.

Was it that she couldn't accept Manny had loved her? Or that she couldn't accept she was wrong?

"It wasn't Manny," Nikki said. "I think he was right all along." And Cooper—despite his instincts—was wrong. "Whoever this stalker is, it's someone you know. Someone who knows you. That's who gave Setters the story."

"And the photos?" Teddie asked, and she sounded almost hopeful that Nikki had an explanation.

But she could only shrug. "I don't know. Manny said the door was unlocked when he first showed up at the cabin. The stalker had been inside. Maybe he hid a camera in there." Nikki kicked herself now that she hadn't looked for one when she'd arrived at the cabin.

That could have been how the stalker had known she wasn't Teddie when she'd left. Maybe he'd had a live feed somewhere inside the cabin. Nikki shivered as it all began to make sense.

"I know you don't trust us," Nikki said.

"You don't trust me, either," Teddie said. "You think I would do this—put so many people in danger—just for publicity? Hell, I could have dated one of those rock stars or movie stars if that was all I wanted. I didn't need to burn down the cabin I loved. I didn't need to…"

"To what?" Nikki asked.

Teddie only shook her head, unwilling to admit what else had happened.

Nikki suspected parts of the news story had been true. Teddie and Manny had crossed the line from protection to passion.

"We were wrong," Nikki admitted. Mostly Cooper. And she couldn't wait to tell him. "But so were you."

Teddie wasn't just wrong, though. She was still in danger.

Chapter 24

She was wrong.

Teddie had made a horrible mistake.

Feeling sick, she stared down at the bits of metal and melted plastic and glass that a fire inspector had sealed into an evidence bag. She was staring at her phone, though, and the photo she'd taken of it. The fire inspector had kept the evidence.

"Looks like a camera," he'd told her. *"Not sure where it was."*

She knew where it had been and what photos it had taken—the ones she had accused Manny of selling to Bernard Setters. She flinched as she remembered all the horrible accusations she'd hurled at him, all the insulting things she'd said to the man she loved and should have trusted.

He would never forgive her.

And she would never forgive herself. How could she have said those things? How could she have been so mean?

Tears stung her eyes, and she blinked furiously to keep them back. She had already cried so many tears over Manny. But then she'd been crying because she had thought he had betrayed her. Now she realized she was the one who had betrayed him.

She picked up the phone with which she'd taken the picture of that evidence bag.

Evidence of her stupidity…

She flipped the screen to her call log. She wanted to call Manny. She wanted to apologize. But she didn't even have his number. The only Payne Protection Agency number that came up as she scrolled was for Cooper Payne.

But if she called Cooper, he might just think she was pulling another stunt for publicity. He doubted her now, like she'd doubted Manny.

And he had every right. How could she have been so stupid? She'd fallen right in with her stalker's plan, just like he had known she would.

Manny had been right about that, too. Whoever the stalker was, he was someone she knew.

Someone who knew her—very well.

She shivered.

Despite its small size, the log cabin was cold. But she was reluctant to start a fire in the hearth. It would remind her too much of the fire that could have claimed her life and Manny's. But her bodyguard had saved them both.

She couldn't count on him to save her again. Not only had she fired Payne Protection but she had also alienated Manny with her insults, with her accusations. The cell screen blurred before her eyes.

But she knew the number she needed to call, the one she always called whenever she needed to talk to someone. Her mother...

Mama would say she'd told her so because Mama hadn't believed that the bodyguard would betray her.

"Stop judging every man by how your father treated me," she'd told her. *"Not every man is a dog. Your Manny sounds like a man of his word. A man of honor and integrity."*

He was—a man of honor and integrity. He wasn't *her* Manny. And now he would never be. Her heart ached over all the things she'd said to him, how she'd accused him of being a criminal like his family.

But she'd done far worse than that. She'd lied to him. She'd told him that she'd only been using him when they'd had sex.

She remembered how he'd flinched when she'd said that. He'd looked like she'd hit him. She hated herself for how cruel she'd been.

She pressed the contact for her mother but nothing happened. She blinked the tears away and looked down at the screen. She had no signal. This cabin she'd found in the UP was even more remote than the one that had burned.

She had needed to get as far from the paparazzi as possible. And she hadn't wanted to see anyone who might tip them off. So she had no neighbors. There wasn't even a town anywhere in the vicinity.

She was as off the grid as she could get. Too far off, she realized now, because she couldn't call for help.

And she suspected she would need it. No matter where she'd gone before, her stalker had always found her.

She suspected he had again, because when she shivered this time it had nothing to do with the cold. She had that feeling she'd lived with for so long—that sensation of being watched.

The stalker had found her.

This was ridiculous. He had put his career on hold for her. His life…

Did she not understand the sacrifices he'd made for her? For years Anthony Esch had been a sought-after fashion photographer. Despite his young age, he'd been working in the industry a long time and had gained a reputation for himself, not just as the son of two world-famous fashion designers.

Mother and Father had started him in his career. But he had earned the respect of other designers, probably even more than he'd gained his parents' respect. They'd always thought him a little inferior because they didn't consider him as creative and artistic as they were.

He should have shown them the photos he'd taken of Teddie and the things he'd done to those photos after he'd taken them. But then they would have sent him back to that *resort* they'd sent him to when he was a teenager.

He snorted. There had been nothing *resort*-like about the rehab facility. He hadn't been there for drugs or alcohol, though. He didn't even like taking the drugs he'd been prescribed.

That was why he'd tossed them all out.

Why did she keep making everything so hard? She

kept running off to these remote places. Or hiring bodyguards.

He smirked. The bodyguards were all gone now. His plan had worked brilliantly.

But his smirk slid away as he remembered the photos he'd seen—the way she'd been with Jordan Mannes. She had never been that way with him. She'd never initiated a kiss. And when he'd kissed her...

There had been no passion. How could she find that uncouth ex-Marine more attractive than him?

Was she blind?

He knew for certain she was stupid. She'd fallen so easily for all his lines. And for his plan.

He'd been outside her building when the bodyguard had stumbled out. The tough guy had looked beaten. She'd beaten him far more easily than Anthony ever could have. That bodyguard wasn't going to rush to her rescue again.

So Anthony had all the time he needed to make her pay for how she'd treated him.

He stared at the little log cabin. This one was smaller than the first one. Just one floor—probably just one room. She'd kept the door locked and the curtains drawn, so he hadn't been able to look inside yet.

But he would soon.

He would be inside with her.

And when he was done, well, this cabin would burn down even faster than the other one. Then there would be nothing left of Teddie Plummer but ashes.

Penny Payne-Lynch had given her son the correct advice when she'd told him to trust his gut. Of course Cooper had been wrong about Teddie. But when Cooper had told Manny what his mother had said, Manny had taken her advice to heart.

Ever since he'd seen that photo of Anthony Esch, his gut had been telling him that Teddie's photographer ex-boyfriend was the guy. He was the right height. The right build. And there had been something in his eyes.

Manny shuddered.

Something cold and just a little inhuman.

Nobody else had noticed it. Everyone else had probably thought Manny was just jealous that the woman he liked had once dated someone that good-looking. But it wasn't how Esch had looked to everyone else that had unnerved Manny. It was how he'd looked at everyone—out of that picture. Like he was above them.

Smarter than them.

Better than them.

Her stalker obviously thought the same thing. That he was smarter than them. Better than them.

And unfortunately, for most of this assignment, he had been.

Until now...

Using some computer skills he'd learned from Nikki, Manny had easily tracked down the proof he needed. It wasn't enough proof to get a warrant issued for his arrest or probably even to convince Teddie of the guy's guilt. But it had been enough proof for Manny.

And for his friends.

Nikki's voice emanated from the headphones Manny wore as he circled over this remote area of the UP, looking for a place to land. It was so heavily wooded that he couldn't find anywhere to put down Cole's plane.

"The fire inspector said Teddie looked at the evidence from the cabin," Nikki told him. "She knows there was a camera planted inside it. So she must know that she was wrong about you."

Manny didn't care about that, not right now. He wanted Teddie to know she'd been wrong about Anthony Esch. He was the danger to her.

What if he just showed up at her cabin?

Would she smile and let him inside? Would she think she was safe just because she knew the guy, because she used to date him?

"It doesn't prove it was his camera," Manny reminded her. They had all been harping at him about not having enough proof for the authorities. So he had had to go after Esch alone.

In addition to being a photographer, the guy was a pilot. He had filed a flight manifest. He was headed to a very remote area of the Upper Peninsula. And he could have only one reason for that: Teddie. He had found her even before Payne Protection had.

He must have planted another camera somewhere. They had searched her penthouse. But what about her mother's house? Esch had broken in there, as well.

Her mother had shot at him. Too damn bad she'd missed.

Teddie was close to her mother. She would have called her mother, would have told her where she was going. Her mother had probably written it down.

He shuddered and hoped he wasn't too late. Where the hell had Esch put down his plane?

Manny was about to put down Cole's brand-new Cessna in Lake Superior. But even if he survived the crash and the icy water, he wouldn't make it to Teddie in time. Esch had too much of a head start on him.

"I might be able to trace the camera back to him,"

Nikki said. "We're getting close to getting enough evidence together to turn over to the authorities. We've got him."

"No, we don't," Manny said. "Not yet."

But he was worried that Anthony Esch might already have Teddie.

What was he doing to her?

How was he hurting her?

The man had terrorized her for months. He was so obsessed, so fixated, that he had to have a plan. Was he going to carry out all the threats he'd sent to her?

His heart pounded nearly out of his chest with a fear more fierce than any he'd felt before.

Manny had thought Teddie had hurt him worse than he'd ever been hurt. But he knew now that he'd been wrong. This hurt more—knowing that she was in danger and not being able to help her. This was torture.

No. This was worse than torture.

He had survived that. He didn't know if he could survive this. He didn't know if he could survive if he didn't reach Teddie in time—if she was already gone when he got to her.

Chapter 25

Because she'd been reluctant to start a fire, Teddie had plugged in the space heater she'd brought up with her. It would have been enough to heat the structure if it hadn't blown a breaker or fuse and plunged her into sudden darkness.

When had it gotten so dark outside?

It was hours ago that she'd had that feeling, that creepy sensation of being watched. But it must have been just her imagination, because when she'd peeked out the curtains, she'd noticed no one outside.

Of course, this area was more heavily wooded than where her previous cabin had been. So her stalker could be out there, hiding behind trees. Waiting for her to come out.

She'd had no intention of going out there until the breaker had blown. Unlike the other cabin, this one didn't have an electrical panel inside the house. All the utilities were enclosed in a small shed that had been built onto the back of the cabin.

Did the shed have a lock? She'd bought a new one for the door and installed it herself. But she couldn't remember if there had been one on the shed. She'd gone inside it to turn on the pump and the water heater and to flip those breakers on when she'd first arrived.

But had she had to unlock the door to access everything?

She shivered as she realized she hadn't.

Anyone could be inside that shed, waiting for her. Maybe the space heater hadn't blown a breaker. Maybe a person had.

The heater had warmed the place enough that she would be fine for the night with a few extra blankets. And as for the lights, she had candles. Using her phone as a flashlight, she found the matches and lit the candles.

They glowed and spread the scent of apple spice throughout the cabin. Losing power wasn't terrible. It certainly was no reason for her to unlock the door and step out into the darkness.

But she should have known the stalker would not give up so easily. He hadn't yet. The knob began to rattle on the door. But the lock held.

He wouldn't be able to break down the door, either. It was made of nearly as thick wood as the log walls.

The windows weren't thick, though. They shattered easily, glass raining onto the floor beneath the drawn curtains. She couldn't see who it was yet. But she wasn't going to stick around to find out. She ran toward the door.

Before she could unlock it, strong hands grabbed her shoulders and whirled her around. And she gasped. But she shouldn't have been shocked.

Manny had figured out who it was. Why had she been so stubborn about what he'd said? About trusting him?

"Anthony?" She shook her head in disbelief. "I don't understand."

He laughed. "Neither did I, Teddie. I didn't understand why you weren't crazy about me. Why you didn't feel what I felt for you."

But that was why she hadn't suspected him— because he had never seemed to feel anything at all. There had been no spark between them, no interest on either part.

She tried to back up, tried to escape him. But the door stopped her short. "I—I didn't think you were attracted to me," she said.

He had never tried anything beyond a couple of chaste good-night kisses.

He touched her face, and his hand shook. "You're beautiful…"

"But there was nothing between us," she reminded him. "No connection."

He grimaced. "Not like you had with that damn bodyguard, huh? How could you find someone that crude—that uneducated—more attractive than me?"

"What are you talking about?" she asked. Maybe she should have humored him or tried to charm him. But anger surged through her at what he'd called the man she loved. "Manny is not crude or uneducated."

He was far smarter than she'd been. How had she never noticed the madness in Anthony Esch's beautiful blue eyes? That was why she hadn't recognized him in the hospital. He must have been wearing dark contacts, and also she had never seen that look in his eyes before.

Anthony sniffed the air like he'd smelled something repulsive. "Of course you would say that. You're just as crude and uneducated."

"How do you…?" Their dates had been awkward and full of long silences. She had never told him the things she'd told Manny about herself.

"You know who I am," he said, full of self-importance. "My parents had you investigated right after our first date. They warned me that you were probably only after my money—or introductions to them."

She'd worked for his parents before. That was how she'd met Anthony. But then she'd only been an employee to them.

She tried to assure him, "I wouldn't use you like that—"

"Like you used Ed Bowers," he interrupted. "He got your career started and you left him. They knew about that."

But nobody knew the whole story. Or at least, they didn't want to believe it.

"And you used your bodyguard," he said, smirking now. "He risked his life over and over again for yours. And yet you so easily believed that he betrayed you." He sighed. "I almost feel sorry for him."

Teddie felt sorry that she would never have the chance to apologize to Manny. She would never have the chance to tell him how much she'd loved him—unless she fought.

She had to fight.

"I didn't use you," she insisted. "I didn't want your money or to meet your parents."

His grip on her shoulders loosened slightly and he studied her face in the candlelight as if trying to determine whether she spoke the truth.

"I wanted to go out with you because you're good-looking," she said, hoping flattery would get her somewhere. It didn't sound as if his parents had ever done much of that with Anthony. "You're talented."

He sucked in a breath and shook his head, as if unwilling to believe her.

"You are," she persisted. "The pictures you take…" She barely refrained from shuddering as she thought of the ones he'd taken recently.

His head bobbed up and down in a series of quick, nervous nods. "Yes, yes, of course, you're right. I am good. I'm really good."

"So don't throw all that away," she encouraged him. "You haven't really hurt anyone." Yet. But now his hands tightened on her shoulders again. "You won't be in any serious trouble…if you leave now."

He laughed. "You don't know."

"What?" she asked. "What don't I know?"

He shook his head. "You don't know what I've already sacrificed for you."

Had he killed someone? Was it too late for him? For Manny?

He'd tried for Manny even when he hadn't been protecting her—probably because he'd known before she had how much the bodyguard had come to mean to her. Just as he'd once told her she'd meant everything to him.

Manny meant everything to her.

"Did you hurt…?" She swallowed hard. "Did you hurt someone?"

"This is all your fault," he said. And now he jerked her away from the door.

Maybe she could get to the window, though—to the one he'd already broken. She wasn't giving up.

"What did I do?" she asked, hoping to distract him.

"You hired that damn Payne Protection Agency."

Oh no. He had hurt one of them. Manny?

Her heart pounded harder now with fear, not for herself but for her bodyguard lover.

"They're not going to stop," he said.

"I fired them," she said. "They're gone."

He shook his head. "They're looking into me. Talking to people about me. The truth is going to come out." He shuddered. "And my parents…"

"They'll understand," she assured him.

He laughed now—bitterly. "You don't know them. They won't understand at all. They'll punish me."

"Anthony—"

"So I need to punish you." He moved his hands from her shoulders to her neck. He slid his fingers around and began to squeeze.

She clawed at his hands, trying to get his hold to loosen. And, remembering the moves Nikki had taught her in the Payne Protection conference room, she lifted her leg and kneed him as hard as she could in the groin.

With a howl of pain, he dropped to his knees.

She gasped at his loosened hold and turned toward the window. But he caught her hair in his hand and jerked her back. "You're not going anywhere," he said.

And something cold pressed against her temple.

He still had the gun he'd taken off Dane Sutton.

She shook her head. "You don't have any bullets," she said. "You fired them all at Manny."

He pointed the barrel at the other window and fired. Glass shattered all around them. "I got more…"

And Teddie lost all hope. She would never get the chance to tell Manny that she'd been wrong, about everything—except falling in love with him. That had been the smartest thing she'd ever done.

Tears burned her eyes, blurring her vision. So she wasn't sure if she was only imagining the curtains rustling at one of the broken windows. If the fabric really was moving, it must have been because of the wind.

But then why was only one set of curtains moving instead of both?

Someone was out there. Someone had come to her rescue. And as her pulse quickened, she realized who it was. But she didn't feel relieved, because she wasn't the only one who'd noticed those curtains rustling.

Anthony swung the barrel of Dane's gun toward those curtains. So, no, Teddie wasn't relieved. She was terrified that she was going to die, and she would have to watch the man she loved die, as well.

The son of a bitch had a loaded gun. Manny had heard the blast. And his heart pounded madly as fear overwhelmed him. Had he shot her already?

Was he too late to save the woman he loved? He pushed the curtains aside and jumped through the broken window. Jagged glass caught at his clothes, cutting him. But that wasn't what hurt most.

A blast rang out, and something tore through his arm. Pain radiated out. But he ignored it and the ringing in his ears.

All he could hear was Teddie's scream.

Candles illuminated the space clearly enough that he could see Anthony Esch, on his knees on the floor— one hand in Teddie's hair, the other gripping the gun. He raised the barrel toward Manny again.

And Manny raised his. Another shot rang out.

And another.

But Manny was squeezing the trigger, too. And he was a better shot.

Anthony Esch stared up at him, his eyes wide with shock over the bullet in his forehead. Then he fell back onto the floor.

Teddie kept screaming.

Had she been hurt?

Manny tried to focus on her, but his vision began to blur. And the gun dropped from his hand as something warm and thick ran down his arm from his throbbing shoulder. "Are you all right?" he asked her. "Did he hurt you?"

But he was the one on the ground now, lying on the floor. He stared up at her, trying to determine if she'd been hurt. Had Esch touched her?

It had taken Manny so long to get to her. Too long…

He reached up and skimmed his fingertips across her jaw. Tears dropped from her eyes and fell onto his face like droplets of rain. "Teddie," he murmured.

Her lips moved, but he couldn't hear what she said. There was a roaring, buzzing noise in his ears, deafening him. Then he couldn't see her lips. His vision blurred, then went completely black as he lost consciousness.

Cooper had known someone was going to get hurt. He'd even figured it would be Manny. But he'd thought the guy was just going to lose his heart.

Not his life, too.

He paced the hallway of the small Northern Michigan hospital. The waiting room was crowded, so crowded that he hadn't been able to breathe in there. He also hadn't been able to face Teddie Plummer.

But now he didn't have a choice because she stepped out into the hall with him, leaned back against the wall and slid down it to the floor.

He dropped to his knees beside her. "Are you okay?"

Back at the cabin, she had refused medical help. All her concern had been for Manny, who'd lain bleeding on the floor when Cooper and the others had arrived. Cole had found a helicopter to make the trip north.

If he hadn't…

Manny might have already bled out on that cabin floor.

Teddie had done what she could to stop the bleeding. She'd ripped towels and wrapped them around his bleeding bicep and another around the bleeding shoulder of his other arm.

Before killing Esch, Manny had taken two bullets. At least…

Maybe the surgeon had found more. They'd had him in the operating room for a while now. Too long.

Teddie must have been thinking the same thing. Tears streamed down her face, and her shoulders shook as sobs racked her body.

Cooper pulled her into his arms and held her like he would have his sister. But Nikki rarely cried. She was the toughest woman he knew. From what he'd seen at the cabin, Teddie Plummer was pretty damn tough, too.

"I'm sorry," he said.

She gasped and stared up at him through her tears. "Oh no! You heard from the doctors? He didn't make it?"

"No, no," he said. "I haven't. Nobody's updated me."

She sagged against him. "Oh, I thought…"

"I know," he said. "I'm sorry about that, too. But I was apologizing because of what I said, what I thought."

She blinked and focused on his face, as if she were trying to figure out what he was talking about. Then she nodded. "You thought it was all a publicity stunt."

"I was wrong," he said. And he should have known that he was. Manny didn't have his family's judgment. He wouldn't have fallen for a woman who'd just been using him.

"I was wrong, too," she said. "About Manny." Her voice cracked with emotion. "Do you think I'll get the chance to apologize to him?"

Cooper nodded. "Of course. Manny's tough. It would take more than a couple of bullets to take him down." He hoped like hell he was right this time.

Chapter 26

Cooper Payne had been wrong before—about her. Teddie hadn't held her breath that he would be right about Manny. He had known the Marine longer than he'd known her, though. So when the surgeon finally walked into the waiting room—where she and Cooper had returned to sit with Lars and Nikki, Dane and Cole—he had good news.

Manny had survived surgery. But due to the amount of blood he'd lost, the next few hours would be touch and go.

"That's my fault," she murmured, more to herself than the others. "I didn't do enough to stop the bleeding." If only she'd moved faster...

But she'd been so stunned over what had happened. How had Manny found her in time? How had he saved her even when he'd been shot?

She had struggled to believe for a moment that any of it was real. That it had actually happened. But Anthony lay dead on one side of her and Manny lay bleeding on the other. So she'd snapped out of her stupor of shock and had done what she could to stop the bleeding.

Nikki squeezed her hand. Her other arm was wrapped around her enormous fiancé's waist. "He's going to be okay," she assured Teddie. She sounded much more confident than her brother had.

Leaning slightly on his petite fiancée, Lars nodded and agreed, "Manny's tough. He'll be fine."

"Can we see him?" Cole asked the surgeon, his jaw rigid with tension.

"Are you family?" the older man asked.

Cole nodded and fingered the dog tags around his neck. "Closer than family."

The guy hesitated but then murmured, *"Semper fi."*

He must have been a Marine, too.

"We put him in a private room, but it's small and he's hooked up to a lot of machines." The surgeon looked at all of them. "If something happens, we need to be able to get in there and work on him. So only one visitor at a time."

Teddie swallowed hard as she considered the implications of his warning. He seemed to expect something to go wrong, to expect Manny to need help. He said nothing more to them, just turned and walked back to the door through which he'd entered the waiting room.

Manny's friends watched him walk away, as well, before they all turned to each other.

"Let Teddie go first," Nikki said.

But Cole shook his head. "Not after the way she treated him…"

Teddie flinched. But she should have known Manny's friends wouldn't easily forgive her. They were all too loyal to brush aside her vicious accusations.

"She was deliberately misled," Nikki said. "Anthony Esch set up the whole thing to get her to fire us." She turned toward Cole. "And you didn't wonder for just a second?"

Cole shook his head. "Not even a second. While Manny likes to talk, he doesn't tell everything he knows. And if he'd wanted to sell a story to the press, he could have made a hell of a lot more off mine."

Who was Cole Bentler? Really? He was more than a bodyguard. More than an ex-Marine.

Teddie didn't really care who he was. She cared about only Manny. But these were his friends. No, they were his family. She wanted to be a part of Manny's life, so she would need to be a part of theirs, as well. She didn't have to worry about just them accepting her. She had to worry about Manny.

"I should have trusted him. I had no reason to doubt him." But fear. She'd fallen so hard and so fast for him that she'd questioned her judgment. "I'm sorry."

"It's not us you owe the apology to," Cole said. "Go ahead." He squeezed her shoulder before nudging her toward the door. "Go see him."

When she walked into Manny's room, Teddie didn't know if Cole had rewarded her or punished her. Seeing the man she loved like this…

Hooked up to machines. It was almost as bad as when she'd been struggling to stop his bleeding. Her knees shook as she approached the bed.

A nurse glanced up from studying the machines. Then she unhooked a couple and pushed them back from his bed. "He won't need these anymore."

Teddie gasped, and her knees nearly folded beneath her. Was she too late? This was what she'd worried about falling for a bodyguard, that one day she would lose him, that he would abandon her just like her father had. "Oh no..."

"He doesn't need them because he's doing so well," the woman said. "He's breathing on his own and already beginning to surface from the anesthesia, which is surprising considering how long he'd been under for surgery." She reached across his bed and squeezed Teddie's hand—like Nikki had. "You came back just in time. I think he'll be waking up soon."

Teddie's heart flipped in her chest as if it was doing cartwheels. "He'll be all right."

Despite the good news, tears streamed down her face. She couldn't believe how close she'd come to losing him. Not that she would have him even if he fully recovered. He would probably never forgive her for the things she'd said, the things she'd believed of him—and she didn't blame him.

But at least he was alive.

Nothing else truly mattered.

The nurse smiled and stepped out of the room. For a moment Teddie felt the panic she'd had back at the cabin when she'd been alone with Manny and unable to help him. Her biggest fear had been of losing him; that was why she'd fought her feelings for him.

But he was going to be fine.

Everyone had assured her that he was tough, that he could survive anything. She didn't need to worry about him abandoning her because of the job he loved. She didn't have to worry that he would ever come up against an assignment he couldn't handle. But she needed him to forgive her for what she'd said to him, for how she'd doubted him. She needed to hear it from his lips, needed to feel his lips again—moving over hers—to believe that they would be fine. She needed to be close to him.

So she pulled down the railing and squeezed onto the bed beside him, careful not to jostle him. But his eyes opened anyway. He turned his head slightly and stared at her. While he was awake, he didn't look fully conscious. He looked dazed. Out of it…

Had the loss of blood caused damage to his brain? Did he not remember who she was?

Or did he not want to remember?

"I'm sorry," she murmured. "So sorry I doubted you. I should have known you—of all people—would never do anything to hurt me."

He cleared his throat and, through dry lips, asked her, "Why not?"

A smile tugged at her lips. "Because you're my bodyguard."

He moved his head, rolling it back and forth across the pillow as if shaking it. "You fired me," he reminded her. He had definitely not forgotten anything. "I'm not your bodyguard anymore."

"No," she agreed. "You're not my bodyguard anymore. I don't think you were ever *just* my bodyguard, though." She reached out and skimmed her fingertips along his strong jaw. The stubble of his new beard tickled her skin.

"What was I, Teddie?" he asked.

"My everything," she said. "You were and are my everything."

That would not change even if he wasn't able to forgive her. She would always love him. She opened her mouth to give him those words, as well, to tell him that she loved him, but he started laughing.

And panic clutched her again, squeezing her heart. She had expected him to be angry. She hadn't expected him to be amused.

Had she read the entire situation between them wrong? Had he only been doing his job when he had saved her life over and over again?

He was dead. Manny had no doubt about that now. There was no way he could be alive and be this happy. Teddie Plummer—his longtime fantasy crush—could not be lying beside him, telling him that he was everything to her.

Manny had never been everything for anyone. Not his family. Not his friends...

He laughed harder, but it rang hollowly off the walls of the small room. Where the hell was he?

This didn't look like hell. Or heaven.

She did, though. Even with her red hair tangled around her face and the dark circles rimming her green eyes, she looked like heaven. Like an angel.

He shook his head as his laughter died away. But was she real?

"I'm sorry, Manny," she murmured, and tears glistened in those beautiful green eyes. "I'm sorry."

For what? He couldn't remember why she would owe him an apology. She hadn't shot him. That had been Anthony Esch...

He tensed for a moment, worried that the man might come after her again. Then a memory flashed through his painkiller-addled mind. Esch with a bullet in his forehead.

The demented photographer would never hurt Teddie again.

She was safe. She was also sad.

"I never meant to hurt you," she murmured. "I love you."

No. This wasn't real. He shook his head and murmured, "What kind of sick joke is this?"

If he wasn't dead, then it must have been the painkillers making him hallucinate and imagine what she was saying. She couldn't actually...

It wasn't possible.

"I'm sorry," she said again, and her voice cracked with the tears overflowing her eyes. "I wish you could forgive me." She began to slide off the bed.

But he grabbed for her, flinching as he moved his wounded arm. And he knew it was real—the pain and the happiness. "Oh, my God," he murmured. "I can't believe this."

"That I'm apologizing?" she asked.

"I can't believe you're real," he said. "I can't believe this is actually happening—any of it."

She relaxed against his side and pressed her lips to his cheek. "It's real. I'm real."

"I had the biggest crush on you when I was younger. I even brought your poster to boot camp," he confessed. "You were my fantasy woman."

"You never told me that," she said.

"I figured you'd think I was your stalker," he admitted, "if you knew about the crush I used to have on you."

"Used to?" she asked. "Not anymore?"

"No, not for a while."

She flinched now. "Not since I accused you of selling me out?"

"Oh, I still had a crush on you then," he said. "I understand why you would have thought that—the pictures, the story. You must have told him the same things you told me." No wonder he'd been so jealous of the guy.

She shook her head. "I only told you about my past," she said. "He knew because his parents had me investigated when we started dating."

She ran her fingertips along his jaw and tipped his face toward her. Staring deeply into his eyes, she assured him, "That's all we did. Just a few dinner dates. I have never felt about anyone the way I do you. I never trusted anyone the way I do you."

And she'd thought he had betrayed that trust. "I would never do anything to hurt you," he promised.

"I know." She blinked back tears, clearing the moisture from her eyes. "Now, about this crush…"

"I don't have a crush on you anymore," he said. "Now I love you."

"Damn it," she murmured.

"What?" She'd professed her love. Had she not wanted him to reciprocate her feelings? "What's wrong?"

She sighed. "Now I'm going to have to tell my mother she was right about you."

"What?" he asked. "Mothers hate me."

"Not my mother," she said. "She loved you from the

minute you first told her off. She was certain you're a man I could trust—with my life and with my heart."

"I am," he promised her. "I will never let you down. I will always be there for you."

She smiled. "I know. Two bullets didn't stop you from saving my life. You are the one who seems like a fantasy to me," his fantasy woman told him. "You're the one who seems too good to be true."

He knew it wasn't just the painkillers anymore. This was really happening. His dream had come true. "We're both real," he assured her. "And what we have is real."

A love that would last forever.

Cole leaned against the door to Manny's room. He wasn't eavesdropping—not really. It wasn't as if he could hear the words Teddie and his friend spoke to each other. But he could hear the happiness. Hell, he could feel the happiness; it flowed under the door and into the hall.

A nurse walked toward the door but stopped short to stare up at him. "I need to check on my patient," she said.

He shook his head. "He's doing great," he assured her. Better than Manny had ever been.

The nurse smiled. "The redhead still in there?"

He nodded, and she turned and walked away. Like Cole, she knew her patient was doing well.

Moments later Nikki appeared in the hall. Her brow furrowed as she stared at him leaning against the door. "Teddie's still in there?"

He had come back a while ago to take his turn visiting Manny. But he hadn't had the heart to interrupt them. Hell, he knew Manny would rather be with Teddie than with any of them.

"Is everything okay?" Nikki asked.

"It's great," he assured her. "In fact, I think you should give your mother a call."

"Cooper called to let her know Manny's going to be okay."

"You should give her a heads-up that she's probably going to have another wedding to plan soon," he said.

Her lips curved into a slight grin and she teased, "Yours? Why, Cole, I didn't even know you were seeing anyone."

He wasn't. He wouldn't.

"Funny," he said. And usually Nikki was, but this time her teasing had struck a nerve. "You know the wedding your mother will be planning next."

"Good thing Mom has Emilia helping her," Nikki said as she leaned against the wall next to Cole. "She has my wedding to plan—although I suspect she's had that all figured out since the minute the doctor told her I was a girl." She shuddered, then shrugged. "Dane's going to pop the question soon."

Cole nodded. He'd seen the ring.

"And what?" she asked. "You think Manny's proposing now?"

"I wouldn't be surprised," Cole said. "He's had a crush on her as long as I've known him."

"She loves him, too," Nikki said. "What about you?"

Cole shrugged. "I'm kind of fond of him. But love…"

She giggled. "You know what I mean. All your friends have fallen in love. What about you?"

Cole had fallen—a long time ago. But unlike Manny, things had not worked out with Cole's teenage crush. Instead of returning his love like Teddie returned Manny's, Cole's crush had crushed him.

He was not about to risk his heart again.

"Not happening," he told her. "There's gotta be one bachelor in every group, you know. I'm going to be that guy."

Nikki snorted. "Yeah, I think that's what Manny said. And Dane. And Lars…"

A chill chased down Cole's spine as he remembered each of his friends making that claim, that they would never fall in love. But his situation was different than theirs. They'd never been in love before. So they hadn't seen it coming.

Cole had been in love.

He'd already given his heart to a woman. And even though she hadn't wanted it, she'd never given it back. So he could not fall in love again. He was safe.

* * * * *

MILLS & BOON®

A sneak peek at next month's titles...

Just can't wait?
Buy our books online before they hit the shops!
www.millsandboon.co.uk

Also available as eBooks.

LET'S TALK
Romance

For exclusive extracts, competitions
and special offers, find us online:

f facebook.com/millsandboon

⊙ @millsandboonuk

𝕏 @millsandboon

Or get in touch on 0844 844 1351*

For all the latest titles coming soon, visit
millsandboon.co.uk/nextmonth